AF423328

Dead Beginnings

Volume 3

ISBN: 9798517491374
Text Copyright © 2021 by Alex Apostol
Cover Design Copyright © 2021 Alex Apostol
writeralexapostol.com

Cover Image Copyright © 2015 IStock by Getty Images _www.istockphoto.com_

All rights reserved. No part of this publication may be reproduced, stored in a retrieval system, or transmitted in any form or by any means- electronic, mechanical, photocopy, recording, or any other- except for brief quotations in printed reviews, without the prior written permission of Alex Apostol.

This is a work of fiction. Names, characters, places, and incidents are either products of the author's imagination or are used fictitiously. Any resemblance to actual events, locales or persons, living or dead, are entirely coincidental

For my tough as nails daughter, Charlotte

More Books by Alex Apostol

YA Fantasy
Broken Angel
(Chronicles of a Supernatural Huntsman, book 1)
Earth Angel
(Chronicles of a Supernatural Huntsman, book 2)
Hunted Angel
(Chronicles of a Supernatural Huntsman, book 3)
Wayfare Angel
(Chronicles of a Supernatural Huntsman, book 4)
Rebel Angel **(COMING 2021)**
(Chronicles of a Supernatural Huntsman, book 5)
Chronicles of a Supernatural Huntsman Part 1 (books 1-3)

Zombie Thrillers
Dead Soil (Book 1)
Dead Road (Dead Soil book 2)
Dead Beginnings Volume 1: Lonnie Lands
Dead Beginnings Volume 2: Lee Hickey
It's an Undead Thing (Zooey Zombie Novella Series)

Women's Fiction: Friendship
Girls Like Us

Nonfiction Journals
Novel Notes
Novel Notes Series Edition
This is Me: A Journal of Self-Discovery
Intentional: A Daily Christian Journal
My Writing Journal
My Riding Journals: Memories and Lessons
Homegrown Herbs & Organic Tea Blends Journal

I

It was the bottom of the seventh. The Trojans were down by one run. Luckily, Olivia Darling was next up to bat. Not a single girl on the softball team worried when they saw her dig her heels into the sand and dirt. They all knew they were about to win.

Olivia stepped up to the plate, her bat gripped tightly in her gloved hands. She swirled it through the air, anticipating the swing that would send the ball soaring over the fence. The bat had been her mother's from when she played high school softball back in the seventies. Olivia only pulled it out for important games, like this one.

The ball of her foot ground slowly, deliberately into the sand and clay. It was as if time had slowed to a crawl, but Olivia didn't mind. She wanted to remember each second of it. She didn't want to miss a single cue, a single subtle nod of the head from the pitcher or twitch of the eye that might give something away. Mistakes could not be afforded in this game. She *had* to get a home run. They *had* to win.

Scouts from multiple Indiana colleges were watching; Ball State, Purdue, St. Mary's, and a few Olivia had never even heard of came just to see her. Beads of sweat popped out from her hairline. She took a deep breath in through her nose and released it slowly from between her lips. Fear was not allowed. Only strength and determination.

On instinct her eyes wanted to shift to the stands to see if her dad had shown up like he said he might, or if her mom was even paying attention. Before she even sat down she said she might have to leave early if she got called into work, which was almost always the case during a game. Before she could scan the crowd, though, she stopped herself. No distractions. *Focus. Concentrate.*

The pitcher threw the ball under hand at top speed, whipping it across home plate at perfect level. Olivia put all her force into her narrow hips as she swung, her long brown ponytail whipping round like a lasso. With an echoing crack the bat made contact and sent the ball rocketing up and through the air.

Olivia didn't have to wait and watch. She knew it was out of the park before it ever cleared the fence. With the biggest smile on her blushed lips she jogged around the plates, her two teammates ahead crossing the home plate and cheering her on as she approached.

Olivia slammed into them as they threw their arms around her, jumping up and down.

"You did it!" Maddie shouted, her blonde curls bouncing against her back.

"*We* did it!" Olivia corrected her best friend.

She was pulled this way and that by her teammates in the midst of all the excitement. This was it. They had won the second to last game of the season. Better late than never was the only bitterness she allowed herself. With the new strand of flu on the loose, knocking people down left and right before the country ever knew what hit it, it was a wonder the game ever happened, it got delayed so many times. But it did and Olivia was the star.

After a few minutes the excitement tapered. The Trojans shook hands with the Vikings in good sport and headed out. Olivia, Maddie, and Jennifer walked together to Maddie's mom's van as they always did after a game. Olivia didn't even bother looking for her mother to ride with her. She knew she was gone before her bat ever made contact with the ball on that last one. *Typical*, she thought and then pushed her anger aside. It was too great a moment to be marred by her mother's indifference.

In hushed tones, Jennifer leaned into the two girls. "We're having a celebratory Dune's sledding night down Devil's Slide. You in?" The question was meant for both Olivia and Maddie but her eyes glared intently at Olivia.

Olivia thought for a moment as she walked, her duffel bag of equipment slung over her shoulder. Did she dare ask her mom permission? The last time she asked her to go out and do something fun in the middle of the night she was turned down quicker than she could get the words out. Why, she still had no idea. It was like her mom enjoyed ruining her fun and telling her no when there was absolutely no reason to.

"I can try. I mean, I'll probably have to sneak out, but sure."

Jennifer's blue eyes lit up, crinkling in the corners from her smile. "And will you be inviting that boyfriend of yours, too?" she ask, conspiratorially.

Olivia narrowed her brown eyes and furrowed her thick brow. "Maybe..." she answered slowly. "Why?"

Jennifer and Maddie giggled together.

Maddie's cheeks blushed when Jennifer didn't say anything. "We were thinking maybe you could ask him to invite some of his karate friends along."

"Ohhh," Olivia threw her head back in amusement as she exclaimed. "I see. Use me for my hookups." But really it came as no surprise to her. Jennifer and Maddie had been hinting at wanting to meet Axel's friends for the entire three months she'd been seeing him.

"No, it's just that—" Maddie started to say in her defense, not wanting her friend to feel used, but Olivia cut her off with a raise of her bronzed hand.

"Maddie, it's fine. I'm kidding. Of course I'll ask him. It'll be fun. I need to get out anyway."

"And celebrate!" Jennifer shouted with her fist raised in the air. This elicited cheers from random fan goers and teammates alike in the parking lot.

"It's so cool that you're dating an older guy. I wish I could find an older guy. The ones our age are so immature,"

Jennifer complained as they climbed into the van, without a care for her mom overhearing from the driver's seat.

Jennifer's mom was the type of mom that did anything to make her daughter happy. If her daughter wanted a new shirt, poof there it was the next day. If she wanted to stay out until one in the morning hanging out with whatever new boy she was dating, no problem. She wouldn't even call to check on her. So, of course, she had nothing to say about her sixteen-year-old daughter's wish to date older men.

"We're gonna have such a wild time tonight!" she squealed as the van lurched into motion.

They talked, laughed, and conspired how to get Olivia out of the house the whole way home.

II

That night, Olivia waited until her mom went back to work for her second shift at the diner before she made any kind of move. She was always the one to contend with if Olivia wanted to do anything outside the home. Her dad had no problem letting her run wild in the streets so long as she didn't disturb him napping on her way out.

"I want you to unload the clean dishes from the dishwasher and put the dirty ones in," Miriam said quickly as she rushed to collect her keys and purse and put her shoes on.

"Can't I just do it in the morning? I kind of just want to relax tonight."

"I would love to relax, Liv," her mother said, irritated. "But not only do I have to try to keep up with cleaning up after you and your father, I also have to work sixteen hours at the diner because Stephanie decided to call off again at the last minute and—"

"OK, OK," Olivia cut her off. "I'll do it. No problem."

"Thank you." Her mother said it but there was no sincerity behind it. She was irritated, again. Olivia often wondered how someone could go through life always on edge like her mother did, always bitter and in a bad mood. It just didn't seem worth it. She almost said something but Miriam shut the door before Olivia could formulate what to say.

She stood there staring at the closed door for a moment. Even though her mother got under her skin and seemed to want to keep her from doing anything fun, a part of Olivia missed her and wished she didn't have to go to work so much. Maybe if they had time to let loose and do something fun together without being rushed to go to work or get chores done around the house they would actually enjoy their time together instead of arguing. But Olivia shrugged off the thought. There was no point in wishing for things that would never come true. Her mother would always be rushed and stressed, at home and at work and everywhere else life took her. That was just her nature. And Olivia was tired of being disappointed in hoping it could ever be any different. She turned from the door and went to her room.

Sneaking out wasn't as hard as it should have been. Even though it was only eight at night her dad was already passed out snoring in his recliner in front of the TV. An old episode of MASH was on, providing soft background noises that prevented him from being woken up by the clicking of Olivia closing the door as she left. She exhaled a little huff of laughter over how easy that was. It was less like sneaking out and more just like leaving, like any other teenage girl who wanted to go out at eight at night would. She stood out on the porch and took a deep breath in through her nose and let it out through her lips.

If it was so easy then why was she disappointed? It wasn't like she wanted to get caught or be in trouble with her parents. But then again she did. It was a feeling she couldn't reason away, even to herself. Why did she feel a seething anger inside of her every time she saw her dad sleeping in that chair? Was it really that unfair with how hard he worked, doing twelve hour shifts on and off at the steel mill? If she had to do the physical labor he did every day she would want to curl up and sleep for the other twelve hours she was off too. And yet she was mad at him for it. Again she shrugged. Wondering about it wasn't going to change it, and it wasn't going to change how she felt, so there was no point.

Like a shot, she took off jogging down the sidewalk to a parked car sitting down the road with its lights off. She opened the door, cringing at the echoing creak it made. She shut the door with a slam and turned to the driver smiling.

"Took you long enough," Axel said, though she could tell he was teasing her and not upset.

"Like you care. You're not even looking forward to going," she responded as she leaned over the center console to give him a quick kiss on his soft lips.

As she was about to pull away he reached up to cradle her chin gently between his thumb and forefinger, brushing his lips against her one more time. "This is true, but I *am* happy to see you."

She stared into his beautiful blue eyes that matched his tall black-to-blue Mohawk and was lost in them for just a moment. Across his nose was a splash of faded freckles that made her chest fill with warmth. Realizing she was getting lost, she leaned back and laughed. "Cheeseball. Let's get going. I don't want to hear Jennifer complaining that we're late."

"Aye Aye, Cap'n," he said with a playful wink and a smile that could have charmed the coldest heart.

Olivia's house was a short drive from the Dunes State Park. Maddie and Jennifer both lived only a few houses down from her, but neither wanted Axel to pick them up since they were going to try to get ahold of Jennifer's older cousin to see if he would buy them booze. Every time she asked he always said no, but she never lost hope. She was one determined girl.

Since it was dark and the park was closed, Axel drove along a winding side road that led to a beach with no guarded gate to pay at. He parked his 1992 Accord in the driveway of a large beachfront home and turned off the engine.

Olivia turned to him, her face pinched together in confusion. "We can't park here. This is someone's house! What if they call the cops?"

Axel laughed and then pointed out his window. "Look. All the lights are off. The grass is overgrown. The gravel hasn't been driven on in a long time before I pulled up. This is someone's summer home and they haven't come back this year yet"

Olivia huffed out her nose and rolled her eyes, ready to argue. "And what if they come back tonight, smart guy?"

"I'm guessing these are Illinois folk, and they are on a way stricter lockdown than we are with this whole crazy new flu thing. They're not coming. It's June. They would have come already."

"Whatever. It's your car that's getting towed."

Axel rolled his eyes but playfully in a way that said he loved the spark inside his girlfriend about as loud as eyes could speak.

The two stepped outside and shut their doors quietly. Olivia took a cleansing breath, though it wasn't as refreshing as breathing in the salty air of the ocean. It was hotter than she expected with very little breeze and there was the faint smell of expired fish that clung to the moisture in the air. She took off her lightweight zip up hoodie and tied it around her waist.

"Good idea," Axel said, following suit. He tossed his on the hood of his car without a care.

Olivia took a sidelong glance at him, admiring the tattoos that peeked out from underneath his black tank top. Already she had run her hands over his bare skin, tracing their outlines a dozen times; the two kamas, sharpened like the scythe of the grim reaper, crossed over his left breast, guarding his heart. The ninja star on his right wrist. The words *Is e glòir duais luach* across his upper back. He had told her the last was his family's motto in Gaelic; *glory is the reward of valor*. He took those words very seriously. As her eyes lingered a thrill crept through her body. Axel was oblivious as he stretched his toned arms high over his head and let out a deep sigh.

"We should get moving. I bet they're already there. Jennifer was pretty excited. You told your friends, right?" Olivia started down the driveway and then down the road without looking to see if her boyfriend was following her; she knew he was.

"Yeah, I told them. They said they were going to make a stop at a party first so who knows when they'll actually get here, but they said they were coming."

"So, there's like a fifty-fifty chance they're coming then," she jested.

He laughed and slipped his hand into hers, interlocking their fingers. "Right." Under his other arm he had a round metal sled tucked tight. "Somehow I knew when you invited me to go sand sledding you wouldn't actually bring a sled. We can share this one if you want."

She shoved her shoulder into his playfully. "Kinda hard to sneak out of your house with a giant sled."

They reached the beach and both slipped off their tongs to carry them in their hands. The sand felt cool on Olivia's feet as she wiggled her toes back and forth. The rest of their walk was spent in comfortable silence, staring at the black water lapping at the shoreline in hushed white noise. Olivia felt her soul was at peace in that moment, that there was nothing immediate she wanted or needed, that she was exactly where she was meant to be with who she was meant to be with. She'd never felt that before.

Quickly, she let go of Axel's hand as she pretended to drop her sandals. He bent down at the same time to get them for her but she was quicker.

"Race you!" she shouted and took off into the dark.

It was a tie when they both reached the Devil's Slide by the main parking lot of the park. Axel interlocked his fingers behind his head, trying to catch his breath.

"You are quick, girl," he huffed.

Olivia chuckled, invigorated. "Too quick for you."

Just then, Jennifer and Maddie walked up. Jennifer had her arms folded over her chest while Maddie carried both their sleds. Olivia thought about asking what was wrong but she already knew; she was disappointed about not getting the booze.

"Well, it's going to be another lame night in Northwest Indiana," she said with a sigh, but then her eyes landed on Axel and her spirits lifted visibly. Her eyes sparkled and she stood a little straighter, her arms unfolding so her fingers could writhe together in excitement. "Hi, Axel," she said in a breathy girlish voice as the blood rushed to her cheeks.

Olivia rolled her eyes. It was pathetic is what it was. Axel was *her* boyfriend. She was standing right there. And yet there was her supposed friend Jennifer gawking at him like a schoolgirl. But then Olivia softened and smiled. Could she really blame Jennifer? He *was* gorgeous.

"Convince any of your friends to come out tonight?" Her voice came out in anticipatory squeaks.

Axel cocked his head and stared directly into Jennifer's eyes, knowing it made her not only excited but uncomfortable. "They'll be here. They just had to make a quick stop at a party first." he said coolly.

She giggled nervously. "Oh, good!"

Axel had a reputation in their small town that even the kids years apart from him in school knew. He was a black belt in karate, lean and mean looking when he wanted to be, and not especially chatty. Rumors flew about how bad he was and all the outlandish things he'd done, all of which weren't true but he never once spoke up against them. When Olivia asked him about it he said he didn't care what people thought. He said there was no point in arguing with ignorant people because he knew exactly who he was.

Before a moment of silence could fall between the friends Maddie stood up straight and spoke up with assurance. "So, Axel, tell me, why *did* you graduate so late? Were you held back?"

"Maddie!" Olivia hissed at her best friend, nudging her with her shoulder for good measure.

"What?" her friend barked back with a shrug. "I want to know."

Axel shoved his hands into the pockets of his black athletic pants and looked at the ground just a second longer than he should have. He sniffed abruptly and shook his head. "No, it's OK," he assured Olivia, knowing she was only trying to protect him because she knew the truth of his history, one he didn't tell often. "When I was three I was diagnosed with cancer, lymphoma. I went through a lot of treatment for the next two years and wasn't able to start school like everyone else. Nothing nefarious."

Olivia jumped in, "And when he was six he was declared cancer free and able to start kindergarten. That's why he graduated when he was nineteen last year instead of eighteen."

"Wow," Maddie breathed out as her blue eyes turned down, her brow furrowed in sympathy. "I'm so sorry."

Again, Axel shook his head and laughed it off. "It's fine. Really. It's the million dollar question everyone's dying to know the answer to about me."

"It's just different is all," Maddie said quietly, shame blushing every inch of her suntanned face. "Usually when you think of someone who's been held back you think of some pothead or derelict who could care less about their education. Just wanted to make sure Olivia wasn't falling in with the wrong crowd. It's my job as best friend to do so."

Axel gave her a nod with a toothless grin of approval that stretched across his cheeks, creating a small dimple on one side.

"But it's pretty amazing!" Jennifer piped up with a smile that split her pretty face in two. "You started off as this sick kid and you ended up this big, tough…man." She stumbled over the last word as if it were foreign, never having referred to any of the boys she hung around with as men before. "I mean, a black belt in karate is pretty impressive under normal circumstances. But you beat cancer too? That's just…wow!"

He gave another shy snort of laughter as he stared down at his shuffling feet. Olivia noticed the movement of his hands in his pockets, his fingers fidgeting uncomfortably. It was not a time in his life he liked to return to. He didn't want to think about who he used to be or how weak he was before. All he wanted to focus on was getting stronger, faster, smarter; on his future.

A small breeze blew off the lake and rustled Olivia's long, stick straight hair that hung like a blanket down to her waist. She pushed it back behind her shoulders and looked up at the tree line at the top of the Devil's Slide. A twig snapped and she narrowed her eyes to focus in on what could have caused it while her two friends chatted idly in hushed tones. Something moved up there but she couldn't be sure what it was. It was too big to be raccoon or a coyote, but too small to be a bear. She wasn't even sure if there were bears in Northwest Indiana, but she was going to guess there weren't. She concluded it was probably a deer and turned her attention back to her friends.

"So if your friends went to a party why didn't you go with them?" Maddie pried some more into the inner workings of Axel Legend.

Finally, he took his hands out of his pocket and folded his arms across his chest. "Parties aren't really my thing."

Jennifer couldn't help laughing at this as she whipped her hair around excessively in an attempt to capture Axel's attention. "Everyone loves parties! What's not to love?"

"Mostly the drinking underage and the potential for getting arrested and having my entire future ruined."

His answer was so blunt, so abrupt, so serious that Olivia couldn't stop the snort that escaped her nostrils as she tried not to laugh. It was the perfect answer that immediately caused Jennifer's pink lips to snap shut in embarrassment. In turn, Olivia couldn't help looking up at her boyfriend in a new light. They had only been going out a few months and with softball season they hadn't spent a whole lot of time together yet; the occasional date or hang out here and there was about all they could muster. She had no idea he didn't like parties or drinking or any of the things all the kids in her school seemed to care about but which she didn't care for at all.

"So if you're not going to ruin your future with arrests then what are you going to do with your life?"

Man, Maddie wasn't going to let up on the interrogation was she? Olivia could hardly blame her. Whenever Maddie had a new boyfriend Olivia did the exact same thing, and at least all the boys Maddie dated had natural colored hair that lay flat on their heads instead of sticking up in sharp points the color of sapphire. It was only to be expected that Maddie would be skeptical of Axel and his intentions with her very dearest of friends.

Maddie and Olivia had been inseparable almost their entire lives. They lived only a few doors down from each other and were in all the same classes since preschool. Immediately, the two were thick as thieves and shared all the same interests; first in coloring, then in gym, then in t-ball, and finally in softball. No matter what was going on in their lives, no matter who they were dating, no matter what their parents did to make them mad, they always had each other to lean on.

Axel didn't hesitate when he answered Maddie's question. "I plan to try pro-fighting for a while before opening my own Martial Arts studio."

"Teaching kids to beat each other up? That's your ultimate life goal?" Maddie shot back without skipping a beat. Olivia saw the little twinge of the corners of her lips that said she was enjoying herself. Olivia nudged her friend in the ribs hard.

None of this bothered Axel in the least. His blue eyes sparkled as they creased in the corners with a sly smile. "Karate is so much more than beating each other up. It's about commitment and hard work and discipline. It's not just about growing your strength or agility, it's about growing your confidence in yourself and in others; things that you can use for the rest of your life in any job anywhere."

"And where will you be opening this dojo?"

"Wherever the wind may take me," he said with his patented charming smile.

"So you don't have everything perfectly planned out then?"

"No," he laughed, releasing the tension that had been hanging in the air. "I'm flexible on location. Here, there, it's all the same to me."

Maddie didn't have a response. She simply nodded her head and gave a smile that told Olivia she was impressed and she approved. It was then that Olivia realized she, too, was impressed with Axel. Sure, he was older than most of the boys she dated but there was something else to him that made him stand out as different and better. He looked like a mother's worst nightmare, but she was realizing he was actually well put together, smart, dependable, hardworking...responsible. Usually that last word turned her off, but in this case it didn't. Before she realized what happened she was picturing herself and Axel on a beach in L.A., the warm breeze drying their salty wet skin, Axel's martial arts studio behind them, Olivia's Team USA Olympic T-shirt clinging to her cool, soaked body.

Reality snapped Olivia back as headlights glared across her face. Quickly, she shifted her gaze from Axel before he noticed she had been staring at him longingly. His friends were there and it was time to get their own party started.

III

Two of Axel's friends from karate hopped out of the beat up, mud-covered Wrangler. They were everything like Axel and at the same time nothing like him. The bigger one was so muscular it tied Olivia's stomach in knots to see the veins popping from his bulging arms. His hair was closely shaved to his head, though she could see it was a brilliant shade of natural red. Freckles splashed his entire face and body as if someone had taken a paint brush and flecked brown paint at him. The other was shorter, leaner, and meaner looking. His face was sharp and angular, like a bird of prey. His green eyes stood out brightly against his pale white skin. Olivia could tell he dyed his hair black because it just didn't look quite right on him; too severe, though she was sure that was the point.

"It's the Legend!" the bird-like one yelled out with his arms thrown up in the air, as if they were long parted friends reunited for the first time and not like they had just seen each other in karate class three hours ago.

"What's up, man?" the redheaded one asked as he lifted a case of beer from the back of his Jeep and shifted it under one arm.

They grabbed hands and bumped shoulders with Axel. Olivia thought it was a weird way of saying hi to someone and imagined what it would look like if she and Maddie were to do it. Her face strained as she stifled her laughter.

"Everyone, this is Brant," Axel said, gesturing to the hulking redhead who was already struggling to grab a beer and open it with one hand. "And this is Samuel." Olivia eyed Samuel suspiciously. Something about his look, the way he carried himself, she could tell he was right on the cusp of twenty-one but not quite there yet. She wondered if his beaked nose could break a board like his fists could.

"What are we doing? Just standing around?" Brant called, his deep voice echoing through the parking lot and getting lost in the trees. Olivia's mind jumped to the shape she'd seen moving at the top of the dune again, but she brushed it aside. "Let's get this party started! Who wants to take on the champ first?" Brant yelled as he held a long black plastic sled high over his head in one hand.

"I'll dethrone the king of the hill!" Jennifer laughed girlishly. She grabbed a can of warm beer from the box still tucked under Brant's arm and cracked it open. The liquid hissed and fizzed as she tipped it back and let it slide down her throat. Olivia snorted under her breath. Jennifer was trying so hard to be whatever this boy wanted her to be, but nothing could hide the wrinkle of her petite nose that said she hated the taste of beer.

Brant, fortunately, was oblivious. "Now we're talkin'!" he crowed before releasing a deep, rumbling belch. He crushed the can he was holding on his forehead and dropped in on the asphalt. Together, he and Jennifer ran up the Devil's Slide.

Axel bent down to pick up the aluminum can his friend discarded without making a show of it and tossed it onto the floor of the open Wrangler. When he turned and saw Olivia staring at him, her lips curling up into a curious smile, he simply shrugged his shoulders and smiled back.

Suddenly, a shriek that could have broke glass emanated from the top of the hill. Olivia whipped around in a fury, her long thick hair flying over one shoulder. Jennifer was sailing down the dune on her silver saucer sled, her hands high in the air as her laughter danced off the leaves of the trees. Brant was barreling behind her, his face pinched stern as if this would help him to go faster. Olivia let out a breath she didn't know she'd been holding.

When they were both at the bottom Jennifer hopped up and bounced around in celebration. Her low cut tank top barely covered her and Olivia worried her breasts would break loose from containment. Brant didn't seem to mind losing his championship title at all as his eyes remained glued on his competitor's body, his mouth hanging slightly ajar.

Axel slapped him on the chest with the back of his hand as he walked by with the sled he'd brought for us to share. "Better luck next time, punk," he laughed. Brant's trance was broken when Axel made contact and he let out a strangled flinch. "Ready to defend your title now, Queen Jennifer?"

She picked up her saucer and narrowed her piercing eyes. "You know it," she growled playfully.

Olivia watched from the bottom, her arms folded over her chest even though she could feel little beads of sweat starting to form on her neck from the summer heat. The two raced each other to the top. It was clear Axel was holding back to keep pace with Jennifer, why Olivia had no idea but she didn't like it.

Maddie sidled over to her bestie and bumped her on the arm with her elbow. "He seems like an all right one," she said quietly. Brant and Samuel were cracking open two more beers and talking low with their heads together, paying them no attention.

"Yeah," Olivia said distractedly, still watching as Axel and Jennifer made it halfway, neck and neck with each other. Axel reached out and shoved playfully at Jennifer's arm eliciting an over-the-top dramatic response that echoed back down to the others waiting. Olivia rolled her eyes.

Maddie followed Olivia's gaze and laughed. "Oh my gosh, you really like him, don't you?"

Olivia furrowed her thick brow. "Maybe. I don't know."

"Yes, you do!" Maddie chuckled and bumped her friend again. "Don't be jealous, girl. He's only playing around with Jennifer like that because he likes you too."

This made Olivia's blood boil up to her cheeks. "So, he's flirting with her to try to get to me?" The very idea enraged her.

Maddie couldn't help rolling her blue eyes at her friend's dullness. "No, dummy. He's acting like he's friends with your friends because he likes you a lot and plans on sticking around. He knows your friends are important to you so he knows he better make a good impression and make friends with them himself."

Olivia turned her gaze back to the two who had now made it to the top of the sand mountain. Jennifer was out of breath doubled over heaving and Axel was laughing so hard his head was thrown back and his hand clutched the lean muscles of his stomach.

"Time's up," she heard Axel call in the distance. "One, two, three, go!"

The two hopped in their sleds with a small running start and shot down the mountain. At first it seemed like it would be a tie until Axel flattened himself against the saucer sled and gained the lead in the last half.

"Maybe you're right," Olivia admitted, her insides cooling off once more. "He *is* pretty great."

"I don't know if I'd go that far, but he's definitely a step up from the usual loser you date."

Olivia turned wide-eyed to her friend, laughter playing at her blushed lips. She shoved Maddie in the shoulder. "Shut up! Like yours have been any better."

"Of course they weren't," Maddie said as she blocked her friend's shove. "That's why I'm not dating them anymore."

Before they knew it Axel was up and standing at their side, his eyes sparkling with curiosity. "You two wouldn't be talking about me, would you?"

Maddie rolled her eyes as Olivia smiled and slid her arms around his waist. "Of course not. You're so into yourself."

He looked down at her with playful shock. "Is that so?" He bent his neck down to plant a soft kiss on her lips, one that sent tingles down her spine and made her knees almost buckle.

"Gross. Get a room!" Maddie said loudly.

Axel didn't comment or retort. He simply removed his lips slowly from Olivia's just far enough to say, "You're up, kiddo. Make me proud."

She shot up onto her tiptoes and planted a hard kiss on his mouth. "As if I could do it any other way."

"Okay, which one of you wants to take on my girl?" Axel called out to his two friends. They were standing a little ways away from the group, just far enough away to not be heard but close enough to feel a part of it all.

"I just cracked open another one, bro," Brant said, holding up the can in his hand as evidence.

"Samuel?" Axel coaxed with a lift of one of his brows.

The bird-like boy heaved a big sigh as if he were being asked to do a chore, but said nothing.

Axel threw his hands up in the air. "Oh, come on, Sammy."

There was a loud belch and then Brant said, "OK, OK," as he threw his head back and chugged his beer. "I'll race the little lady."

"Um," Axel faltered when he took a good look at his friend. Brant had been drinking nonstop since they got there a little more than half an hour ago. There were at least six crushed cans laying at his feet, and that didn't include the one Axel had already tossed in the back of the Jeep. Brant's already catlike eyes were narrowed lazily, his giant boulder-like body swaying a bit if he tried to stay in one spot too long. "I don't know if that's such a good idea, buddy. You've had a lot to drink already."

"So?" Brant barked a little more harshly than he intended. "What are you, my mother?" He snorted a laugh that reminded Olivia of a pig. He belched again, so loud it ran up the hill and through the trees and back again. Thinking this was the greatest thing in the world, Brant doubled over in laughter and then held his hand up for Samuel to high-five. Reluctantly, it was received.

"I don't think you should race him," Axel said low, turning to Olivia.

"Whatever. It's not a big deal. I haven't had anything. What's the worst that could happen? He falls over and I win by default?"

Axel chuckled at the thought. "Not saying I wouldn't like to see that. I just want to make sure you're OK."

"I'll be fine," she promised with a quick peck on the lips. "OK, Brant. Let's do this!"

"WHOO!" the drunk boy cried out like a wolf.

After a few stumbles and some crawling, the big man finally made it to the top where Olivia was waiting. They both sat on their knees, hands holding onto the handles carved out of the sides of the plastic. Olivia had decided to take Jennifer's bright orange toboggan for a spin to match Brant's.

"One, two, three!" Olivia cried as she pushed off the edge.

She flew down the dune at top speed, her long hair trailing behind her in sheets. Brant was right alongside her, his sled looking unsteady as he blinked and tried to force his eyes to focus. Olivia heard cheering at the bottom from Axel and the others. When she heard her name it brought a smile to her face. In that moment she felt loved, important, like she mattered when most of the time she didn't. She liked that feeling. Just as she was getting lost in it Brant leaned too far to the left causing his sled to take a sharp turn right into her path.

With a loud smack, the two collided halfway down the mountain. Because he was drunk, Brant's two hundred pounds was like dead weight hurling itself onto Olivia's one hundred and fifteen pound frame. She felt a sharp pain in her wrist and clutched it to her chest as she tried her best to tuck and roll the rest of the way down. Sand assaulted her eyes and nose and mouth. She tried to spit it out but more came pouring in. It felt like she was drowning and for a moment, in all the confusion, she thought she was. Her body finally came to a halt at the bottom with a thud. She lay sprawled out on her back, right arm still clutched tight to her breast. She sucked in a deep breath and immediately regretted it when the sand that was in her mouth shot down her throat. She sat up quickly and hacked, trying to get the grit to come back up.

In seconds Axel was by her side, his hands roaming her. "Are you OK? Are you all right? Are you hurt?" he asked in a panic, his eyes so wide she thought they were going to bug right out of his head.

She wanted to answer him, but her head hurt and her vision was still spinning from all the somersaults. She opened her mouth, but all that came out was another string of coughs. She spat a wad of sad on the ground and finally she was able to talk again. "I'm fine, I think," she said. Axel grabbed her under her good arm and hoisted her up with ease. "My wrist, though," she started to say but she was cut off.

They all heard the unmistakable sound of tires rolling across the sand-covered asphalt as blue and red lights swirled the night sky.

"Cops, man!" Samuel said, grabbing Brant by the arm and trying to drag him to his feet. "Come on! I'm not getting arrested for your drunk ass!" He yanked and yanked until his lugging friend could stand and he dragged him off to the Jeep. They peeled out without another thought for the others and what they were going to do.

"Get out of here," Olivia ordered Maddie and Jennifer. "Go!"

"Call me later," Maddie pleaded as she turned and ran, looking over her shoulder at her injured friend.

Olivia nodded as she waved her off with her good hand. Axel put his arm around Olivia's shoulder and guided her away from the swirling lights and back to their vehicle parked in the absent strangers' driveway. Once they were in the car they felt safe. But Olivia winced when she tried to buckle her seatbelt.

"Dammit!" she yelled, slamming her other fist on the dashboard. "I have a game tomorrow! *The* game. My last game!"

Axel put a hand on her shoulder as he started the car. "Let's get you to the hospital."

IV

The emergency room was silent, the waiting room void of patients save for one older gentleman and his wife who were sitting closely, each clutching a wad of tissue paper in their hands. When Olivia gave her information at the check-in desk they made it very clear they were going to have to call her parents. She didn't have an insurance card on her and there was no way she was going to take an even worse verbal thrashing when the full bill came in the mail weeks from now. Reluctantly, she gave them the phone number to her mother's work. She figured that would be the better parent to get the call and break the news to the other one, plus her dad was most likely passed out in his chair in front of the TV still. He wouldn't hear the phone if it was attached to a dump truck driving through the living room wall. There was nothing left to do but have a seat and wait.

"You know, you really don't have to stay," Olivia said, offering Axel a way out.

"Of course I do. I want to make sure you're OK, especially since it's my own stupid fault you're here at all." The way he said it made Axel sound defeated, but his face contradicted it. He sat up straight and tall with his chin tilted slightly upward, as if it were his duty to watch over his girlfriend diligently.

"It's not exactly the best first meeting of the parents, though."

Axel shrugged as if those things meant little to him. "They are either willing to give me a chance or not. How and where I meet them has little to do with the matter. At least that's what I've found with parents over the years."

Olivia couldn't help laughing to herself at the way he spoke, as if he were a fifty-year-old man and not a twenty-year-old kid. "Wise beyond your years, you are," she said in her best Yoda voice.

This caused him to break face and snort a small chuckle under his breath. "I just want to take care of you," he said in all seriousness.

Olivia looked up into his striking blue eyes and softened. "I know you do. That's why I love you." The words slipped out without her meaning them to. Her cheeks rushed with blood when she realized she couldn't call them back. Was it true? Did she love Axel? She thought she was beginning to, if what she felt was love. She'd never been in love before, so she wasn't sure. All she knew was that she felt very differently about him than she had about anyone else.

Axel's face froze mid-laugh. He turned to look at her, his lips parted in shock. "You love me?" There was hope in his voice. At least she thought that's what she heard. It definitely didn't sound like disgust or revulsion.

Olivia's eyes fell to her hands that wrung together in her lap, her wrist stinging with each twist and turn. She gave a small wince and placed each hand purposefully on each knee to keep still. With a small shrug of her shoulders she said, "Yeah, I guess I do."

Axel released a cross between a huff of relief and laughter through his nostrils as an uncontrollable smile took over his face. He leaned over and reached for her face, cupping it in his hands gently. "Come here, you," he said as he pulled her lips to his.

It was a perfect moment, one that Olivia hoped she would remember for the rest of her life, one that she could tell to her kids someday as living proof that love really does exist in the world and she'd found it.

"Olivia Ann Darling!" her mother's voice called sternly from across the room.

The entirety of Olivia's body tensed up as she sprung away from her boyfriend. "Mom," she said meekly.

Her mother walked quickly over as they both rose from their seats to stand awkwardly. Well, Olivia stood awkwardly. She would have rather been anywhere else in the world than in that hospital at that moment. Axel stood firmly, his hand resting at his sides confidently, as if there was no one else he could possibly pretend to be other than himself.

Miriam's tired yet frazzled eyes popped over to look Axel up and down in a blink before turning back to her daughter. "What the hell happened?" was the only question she could think to ask. "I get a call from the hospital saying you've checked into the emergency room with a possible broken wrist and my heart just about stopped. I thought you were at home tonight! I didn't know if you were alone or what was going on."

"I wasn't alone, mom," Olivia said, irritation underlying the softness in her tone. "I went out with Maddie and some friends."

Miriam motioned to Axel with wide eyes and a snort. "Yeah, I can see that. Who are you?"

Her tone was sharp enough to cut holes in the poor boy, but Axel didn't falter or hesitate. He stuck his hand out and smiled. Olivia saw the little dimple in his cheek and couldn't help smiling herself, hoping beyond hope that her mother liked him despite the circumstances of their meeting. "I'm Axel, Mrs. Darling. Axel Legend."

"Ah," Miriam said with recognition that he was used to by now. All the parents knew his story, knew of his cancer when he was younger and the hell his parents went through to make sure he survived. It was a small town and people talked. "My daughter's mentioned you, but I didn't know you two were…" She left the end of her sentence hanging for one of them to pick up.

"Dating?" Axel offered, taking his hand back after a quick, forced shake. "It hasn't been long. Only a few months, but yeah we are."

Olivia wanted to crawl under a rock and stay there until she graduated. Her mother wasn't overly grilling Axel, but the way her eyes narrowed when he spoke and the shortness of her answers mortified Olivia to no end. Why couldn't her mother just be nice on the simple fact that she knew Axel was someone important to her? Why couldn't she give him a chance before she disliked him? She could tell Miriam's mind was already made up though, and there was little hope of changing it. Her mother's eyes kept crawling up the spikes of Axel's blue mohawk as if it were a repulsive creature ready to attack them.

"Olivia Darling!" someone called from beside the desk. "You can follow me."

Just then, Olivia's father came strolling up. He had his hand shoved deep into the pockets of his old, rumpled sweatpants. His eyes were still half-closed as if he still hadn't been able to pull himself out of the wonderful nap he'd been enjoying.

"What did I miss?" he asked and then cleared his throat with a raspy cough.

"We're about to find out," Miriam answered, irritation dripping from her tongue.

Olivia turned to Axel. She attempted a smile, though tears gathered in the corners of her eyes. "Thank you for taking care of me."

He smiled back. "Anytime. Call me later and let me know how it goes."

She nodded hoping her upturned lips conveyed the silent apology she felt inside.

It must have because he shook his head slightly as if to say it was no big deal. "It was nice to meet you Mr. and Mrs. Darling."

"Uh huh," Miriam said absently as she herded her family toward the doors to their examination room.

Olivia thought the waiting room meeting of Axel would have been the worst of it, but she had another thing coming once they were behind closed doors. It was just Olivia and Miriam. Her dad was there, but as usual he wasn't really there. He plopped down in his chair, gave a roaring yawn as he stretched his wide arms over his head, and then hunkered down and closed his eyes. Olivia turned to her mom but didn't dare to speak first.

Miriam refused to sit, pacing the room like a caged tiger. She walked with her hands tucked into the pocket of her diner apron, looking at the floor and shaking her head as she muttered to herself. Occasionally, she stopped to look at Olivia, shake her head, and start all over again. It was the slow build up to the inevitable outburst. It was more than Olivia could take. She had to know what kind of trouble she was in. The waiting was excruciating.

"OK, I get it!" she all but yelled as she stood up from the examination table, the tissue paper crinkling under the fury of her movement. "I shouldn't have gone out without telling you. I'm sorry, but I'm sixteen, almost seventeen, and I should be able to live my life and go out with my friends once in a while too." As soon as she closed her mouth she knew she'd only made things worse. Nothing like the old I was wrong but really I wasn't wrong to get a parent going.

Miriam turned to her daughter, one eyebrow raised high on her forehead as she placed her hands firmly on her hips. "Tell me? You should have told me you were going out?! How about asking! You're right, Olivia Ann, you are sixteen. You're *only* sixteen. I have to know where you are and who you're with at all times!"

Olivia's defenses bristled. "Oh, here we go!" she spoke wildly with her hands. "I knew it'd come to this. You're not mad I went out, you're mad about who I was with. You don't like Axel!"

"Like Axel? I don't even know the first thing about this Axel!"

Olivia laughed as she looked at the ceiling, letting her hands slap against her thighs. "*This* Axel? Why do you have to refer to him like that, like he's trash or something?"

Miriam took offense to this and her pinched face showed it. "I didn't. I just meant I don't know him and it doesn't seem like you know him all that well either. But if he's the kind of boy that encourages you to sneak out in the middle of the night to break the law and trespass on state property then I don't think he's the type of person I want you hanging around with."

Olivia couldn't help letting out a howling laugh that echoed off the walls and down the hall despite the door being closed. "Axel influence me? Jennifer is the one who orchestrated the entire night! We just went along because she invited us and it sounded fun. You know, fun? Like what teenagers are supposed to do?"

"Don't take that tone with me, young lady. I don't like you hanging around with him and that's final." Miriam was unsure of the stance she was taking on the situation, which was clear in the way she shifted her weight and pushed at the side of her mouth with her tongue. But it was too late to turn back. She had to stick to her guns.

Olivia let out a groan of agony that only a teenager could conjure up. "You're so ridiculous! You didn't even give him a chance!"

Just then there was a soft knock at the door and it opened just a crack. "Hello, dere," a giant man with shoulder-length wavy dark hair tied back in a ponytail said as he stuck his head in.

He was even larger once he allowed his entire body to fill the doorway. Olivia looked up at him, craning her neck with wide eyes. Was this supposed to be the nurse who was going to take her vitals? He looked more like a prison break out dressed up in costume to avoid capture.

"I just need ta check yer vitals and take a quick look at yer wrist dere and then I'll be outta yer hair."

Olivia couldn't hide the confused surprise on her face as she examined his accent. The nurse let out a laugh, his face brightening with his smile.

"My name is Lee," he said as she held out his hand for her to shake.

She placed her hand in his, feeling its warm and gentle grasp though it was twice the size of her own.

"Where are you from?" Miriam blurted out harshly.

"Mom!" Olivia snapped.

"It's OK. I get dat a lot. I'm from Ireland, Ma'am."

"And you're licensed in the United States?" she fired off without regret or shame.

Olivia was mortified for the second time that night. Her breathing actually stopped as she waited for the rightful outburst from her nurse. Instead, he looked down at his white tennis shoes with a wide grin and laughed under his breath. "Ya, I'm licensed and a professional. I assure ya I will take excellent care of yer daughter, ma'am."

This seemed to satisfy Miriam. She let herself sit down in the seat next to her husband who was softly snoring with his chin touching his chest. She nudged him with her bony elbow and he jostled awake with an irritated grunt.

Lee went through the familiar motions of taking Olivia's temperature and blood pressure, writing it all down on her chart. He then took her wrist gently in his large hands and looked at it, turning this way and that slowly.

"So, why are you just a nurse and not a doctor then? Couldn't finish medical school?" Miriam was irritated with her husband for falling asleep, pissed that she was called out of a double shift, worried about how that made her look to her boss and work friends. It all built up and there was no other target left in the room to take out her anger on than the poor nurse attending Olivia.

"Oh," he said casually, not taking his eyes off his work, "I suppose for tha same reasons you're just a waitress and not a doctor."

Olivia let out a single burst of shocked laughter, her gaze bouncing between Lee and her mother. Did he really just say that? He called her out like it was the easiest thing in the world. Why couldn't she do that?

"If yeh don't mind stepping out for just a moment, ma'am and sir. I'm going ta examine the arm and ask your daughter some questions about what happened," Lee asked with a voice as polite and innocent as a lamb that had not just verbally checked anyone in the room.

"Step out? We are her parents. You can't ask us to step out," Miriam said, not quite yelling but almost there.

The shrill in her voice perked up her husband. He roused himself, rubbing his face with a deep sigh. "Come on, Miriam," he said as if this were common practice. He put his hands on her shoulders and walked her out the door. "I could use a coffee, how about we get one and settle down a bit?"

Once the door was closed Olivia exhaled a deep sigh of relief. "Thanks for that," she said with a smile. "I'm sorry. She's just…" She didn't quite know how to finish that sentence but luckily she didn't have to.

Lee shook his head and waved it off. "Ah, tis nothin'. I'm used ta it." He wheeled his chair in front of her and took her exposed arm in his large hands.

She was surprised at how gentle his touch was for being such a hulking man, like a mother assessing her newborn baby. "Get a lot of crazy parents in here, huh?"

"Actually," Lee said, not taking his eyes off Olivia's arm but raising his eyebrows in hidden amusement. "From my in-laws. They don't like me all tha much. Think I married their daughter for a green card or somethin' like that." He laughed to himself at the ridiculousness of it all.

"That's awful. I'm sorry," was all Olivia could think to say. It was rare that an adult ever opened up to her about something personal in their lives, like they thought if they dared to show that they too had feelings and were real human beings that their control over the kids would crumble and fall apart, when in reality it was the opposite. Having Lee open up to her, even in that little bit, made her see him in a different light than just the hulking nurse man. She had respect for him and could relate to him.

Lee shrugged his shoulders. "Nah, in the grand scheme of things it does no matter all too much. I love my wife and she loves me. Dat is what really matters."

Olivia was taken aback by his honesty. She stared into his dark eyes even though he was again consumed in examining her wrist, turning it this way and that.

"Welp," he said as he pushed back, the clatter of the chair's wheels snapping Olivia out of her head. "Yeh look ta be in good workin' order. I don't think it's broken. How about we give dat mother of yours da good news?"

Olivia laughed and nodded her head. As soon as he popped his head out of the door Miriam and her husband were back in the room standing on each side of Olivia like sentinels, Miriam's arms folded across her chest while her more lax partner sipped on his steaming cup of coffee.

"The bone does no feel broken, just badly bruised. We could take her back for some X-rays if dat'll make yeh feel better, ma'am." He was composed and professional despite having put her in her place moments ago and this threw Miriam off. Olivia could tell by the wrinkle in her brow that she was still ticked off about it.

"Uh, well, yeah. I mean no. That'll be fine. She's fine. We would just like to take her home."

Olivia tried to hide the smile that strained to creep across her lips by lowering her head and staring at her flip flops.

"Very well, ma'am. Good day ta yeh. If yeh wait here someone will be in with da discharge papers."

"Am I clear to play softball?" Olivia asked, finally raising her gaze to catch him before he disappeared into the hallway.

"Well, yer going ta be a wee sore but if yeh go easy I don't see why not."

She was so happy she could have hugged him, but instead she settled for a grand smile and a thank you.

"Best of luck to yeh, little lass," he said with a wink. And just like that the giant nurse, Lee Hickey, was gone from the room and onto helping another patient.

Olivia did all she could to avoid her mother's gaze. She looked at her fingers intertwining, at her bare toes wiggling, the red paint chipping off the edge of her big toe already though the white summer flower painted in the corner held up nicely.

"Let's go," Miriam ordered without another word.

The entire ride home Miriam laid into Olivia about being responsible, about always telling one of them where she was going and who she was with and how she didn't think this Axel was the best influence for her, but Olivia barely heard a word. Her mind was on the game tomorrow. It was another big one. College scouts from out of state schools were coming to see her. This could be her ticket out of Northwest Indiana. Her stomach tied in knots the longer she thought about it but at the same time the smile grew wider on her face as she watched the houses go by outside the window. In her hands she gripped her lucky bat, the one her mother had used when she was younger. In some way, it was the one connection Olivia had to the mother she felt she could relate to. Like that bat was the last living hope of her mother ever understanding her and letting her be who she was meant to be. She'd seen it on the floor and picked it up to lay it across her lap without even thinking, like it was an extension of her that belonged nowhere else but in her hands.

V

The next morning Olivia found herself in much of the same position as she'd been in the night before on the drive home. She sat in the middle row of the minivan, in the captain's chair with her bat clutched in her hands, only this time they were gripping the wood so tightly it almost hurt. They had picked up Maddie, Jennifer, and two other girls on the team and were driving to the game.

"It's going to be great," Maddie offered with a soft touch of her hand on Olivia's arm.

She'd woken up with her wrist feeling a little stiff and almost had a panic attack. It took a few minutes of working out the kinks to make it feel normal again. She was sure the misfortunes of last night would not hinder her performance today.

Jennifer turned around from the front passenger seat. "Yeah, you're a rockstar, girl. You got this!"

"Thanks, guys," Olivia laughed. "Now let's do this!"

Miriam glanced back in the rearview mirror to see her daughter sitting in silent anguish.

"And I'll be right there cheering you on, sweetie," she offered, though the break in her voice told everyone in the van she felt uncomfortable and nervous saying it.

"You're what?" Olivia asked in shock.

"What do you think? I'm going to watch your game."

Olivia looked at her like she had just spontaneously sprouted two heads. "But you never watch my games. You always have to work or do stuff around the house, or *anything* but watch my games."

She could see through the mirror this wounded Miriam a little but her mom tried not to show it. She was always so stoic. "Well, today's different. I'm going to your game, seeing as it's the most important game of your life, right?"

Olivia's face broke open into a goofy grin. "Yeah, right," she agreed, not sure if she felt like laughing or crying.

Suddenly, Miriam slammed on the breaks and the van came to a screeching halt. "Jesus!" she burst out, her breath coming out in ragged huffs.

In the middle of the road was a woman. She was walking along as if she had no idea where she was, but Olivia could tell there was more than dementia inhibiting this lady. Instead of picking up her feet and walking normally she dragged one foot behind her slightly and limped along.

"Is she all right?" Jennifer asked, squinting her eyes for a better look from the front seat.

"I don't know, dear," Miriam answered absently. She was trying to get a better look at the woman herself, but the mysterious woman had her head turned in the wrong direction for anyone to see who she was. She tapped the horn. The quick blare echoed through the empty street.

"Mom!" Olivia said, exasperated.

"What?" Miriam shrugged, her hands still gripping the wheel tightly as her heart finally started to slow back down to it's normal pace. "Maybe she doesn't realize there's a car driving here."

"How could she not?" Maddie asked, unbuckling her seatbelt and leaning forward between the front seats for a better look.

The woman slowly turned, her head first until her body had no choice but to follow. Once she was facing them, they all knew why her head slumped against her shoulder; she had a gaping wound, as if a wild animal had taken a huge bite out of her neck and shoulder leaving the veins and tendons exposed and dripping black blood.

Every female in the van let out an involuntary gasp as they covered their mouths with their hands.

"Oh God!" Jennifer exclaimed as she pointed. "How is she even alive?"

Miriam shook her head. With her mouth hanging agape she said, "I don't know. I don't..." but she was cut off by sudden movement.

"Oh man, she's coming over here!" Maddie screamed.

None of them were sure why they were so terrified of a woman mortally wounded, but they were. An instinct deep inside them told them there was something wrong with this scenario. Olivia could feel her heart beating roughly against her ribs, her chest rising and falling in quick breaths. She was going into flight or fight mode but she had no idea why.

"What do we do, mom?" she asked in almost a whisper as she leaned forward into her mother's ear.

"I don't know, sweetheart. I've never…I just don't know what to do."

Suddenly, there was a loud bang as the woman threw herself onto the passenger side window. Blood smeared the glass as she dragged her hands down it, the squealing of soaked skin against glass causing everyone inside to shudder.

"What the hell? What is she doing?"

"What's going on?"

"What do we do?"

"Is she trying to get in?"

The girls rattled off question after question in their confused panic.

"Will everyone please just shut up and give me a minute!" Miriam yelled. She leaned over the center console towards Jennifer and spoke loudly and slowly to the woman on the other side of the window, though not daring to roll it down. "Can we call for help for you, Miss?"

The woman didn't seem to acknowledge that anyone inside was trying to talk to her; she just kept pawing at the window as if she were trying to claw her way inside, her face slack, her wound weeping, dripping onto the steaming summer pavement.

"Miss? Are you all right? How can we help you? We don't know what to do?"

The woman opened her mouth and everyone seemed to lean forward in anticipation of hearing what she had to say. Her lips parted and all that escaped was a ghastly, guttural growl. Immediately, all the girls scooched as far away from the window as they could get, Jennifer the most since she was the closest.

Without warning, the woman threw her head forward, smashing it into the glass. The force was enough to create a head-size crater with spidering fractures running off. The girls all screamed at the top of their lungs, clutching whatever body was closest to them. The woman leaned back and threw her head forward again. The glass shattered into pieces and fell to the ground in a shower of jagged splinters. The screaming inside grew louder. Jennifer struggled to undo her seatbelt as Olivia and Maddie urged Miriam to step on it and get them out of there, but Miriam was in shock. She knew what she should do but her limbs were frozen in fear.

The woman leaned in and grabbed ahold of Jennifer's neck, tugging her toward the gaping hole that had been a window a moment ago.

"NO!" the teenage girl screamed, clawing and kicking and hitting where she could, though her eyes were squeezed tightly shut. Tears streamed down her face.

Maddie and Olivia unlocked their seatbelts and tried to grab hold of Jennifer's arms, but they were flailing around too wildly for either of them to get a good grip. With inhuman strength, the woman pulled their friend from the passenger seat and threw her to the ground like a sack of grain. Jennifer curled into a ball and covered her face with her hands as the woman descended upon her.

Then came a scream so blood curdling, it was unlike anything they had ever heard before.

Listening to a painful slow death was nothing like it was in the movies. Sure, the actresses put on a good show with as high pitched of a scream as they could muster, but the real thing was more horrifying. There was no faking the sounds that came out of Jennifer in those moments. Blood splattered the side of the van as the woman tore with teeth and nails, shoving whatever she could into her mouth and swallowing without chewing.

"OH GOD!" Miriam screamed, her knuckles white as they gripped the steering wheel, tears streaming down her face.

Another loud thump hit the van, only this time it was in the front. Another person, this one a short man with mangled blonde hair matted with blood, tried to reach over the hood to get at Miriam though his arms were too short to reach. His nails scraped against the van's hood leaving scratch marks in the paint.

"Let's go! Just go!" Maddie and Olivia were screaming in turn, but it did little good. Miriam was in shock, her face streaked with liquid black rivers of mascara and eyeliner.

Without thinking, Olivia reached around and grabbed her bat she'd dropped on the floor. "Come on! We have to get out of here," she said in a commanding tone fit for an officer.

The bite in her voice made Miriam blink. She turned to look her daughter in the eyes and tried to draw strength from them. Olivia was wearing her burgundy school t-shirt embellished with a giant golden Trojan warrior's head. The number forty-one was scrawled across the back with her last name, Darling. Darling forty-one, the Trojan warrior. Just then a terrible pop and hissing joined the snarling that made everyone's heart sink.

"There goes the tires," Maddie sobbed.

"Mom!" Olivia yelled when she saw her mother's vacant eyes staring. "We're almost surrounded. We have to get out of this van and into a house or shelter or something, now!"

Miriam nodded vigorously in agreement and pried her fingers from the steering wheel.

"Maddie and I have our bats. Here," she leaned over the side of her seat and pulled another bat from a golden bag. "You can use...Jennifer's..." Tears collected in the corners of her eyes but she forced them down by sheer willpower. She couldn't afford to lose focus right now. She couldn't afford to have her vision blurred by the memories of her goofy, outgoing, kind-hearted friend who now lay in pieces on the pavement, a bloody mess of gore and scraps and bits.

Miriam took the bat from her daughter and climbed over the center console into the middle seat with them.

"I'll open the door and then we swing and run, got it?"

"That's not much of a plan," Maddie groaned as her sweaty hands gripped the base of her worn bat.

"It's the best plan we've got right now. We can make a break for Axel's house. It's just the next street over, straight through that yard there," she said nodding out the window to the baby blue house across the street from them.

Miriam and Maddie nodded their agreements but both were unable to allow any sound to escape their lips as they trembled.

"One, two…three!" Olivia shouted as she pulled on the handle of the sliding side door, yanking it open.

The sound was enough to attract the attention of every crazed, murderous person in their vicinity.

Olivia shouted motivation. "Go! Go!" she said like the leader of a group of parachuters.

One by one they jumped from the van and made a break for it; Maddie, Miriam, and Olivia bringing up the rear, though she quickly sprinted to the front of the line just in time to whip the end of her bat into the skull of the man who had been trying to get at Miriam through the windshield. A satisfying crunch followed and the man crumpled to the ground in a heap, the side of his head caved in and oozing a steady stream of thick dark blood.

His body went down so fast Maddie had no time to react. Her feet got caught up and she went down with him, falling on his limp form with a thud. Olivia and Miriam were so focused on getting to Axel's house no one noticed what had happened. They reached the sidewalk across the street and heard a piercing cry.

"Olivia!" Maddie shouted from the ground as more surrounded her.

Olivia bolted to her best friend, bat clenched tightly, legs pumping as fast as they could carry her.

"Olivia, help!" Maddie continued to cry as she tried to push herself up from the ground to stand. But just then, the nearest two vicious forms fell on her, dragging her back down as they sank their teeth deep into the soft and tender flesh of her neck and shoulder. Her cry echoed through the deserted street.

Olivia came to a stop and reached out her hand to help her. Their fingertips touched and for a moment there was hope from both of them. But then Maddie was yanked back as the grabbing hands and chomping teeth looked for more flesh to devour. Olivia swung her bat madly but it wasn't enough. There were too many now, more and more coming to fall upon her.

Maddie cried out uncontrollably until there were a dozen surrounding her and the clawed hands tore her throat wide open. She gurgled, choking on the heavy stream of her hot red blood until the life extinguished from her beautiful blue eyes. Olivia saw it all. The beastly people paid no attention to her since their mouths were already full with juicy, fresh, and tender flesh. And then there was silence from her dearest friend. Nothing could be heard except the sickening sound of chewing and tearing. Olivia took one last look into Maddie's tear-filled open eyes.

This time Olivia couldn't talk herself into suppressing her tears. They flowed freely down her bronzed round cheeks as she watched her childhood friend's blond hair turn red, soaked through with her own life's blood.

"Olivia!" she heard her mother cry out from behind her, though she dared not move from the sidewalk that somehow still felt safe. "Olivia, honey, come on!"

With one hand, Olivia wiped the tears from her face and charged off toward her mother, surpassing her without so much as a word. They ran through the yard of the blue house without another encounter but were not so lucky once they reached the driveway. Two kids, newly turned teens, sat on the concrete, lazily dragging pieces of chalk they held loosely in their scratched and beaten hands. They only looked up when they heard Miriam curse the sight of them.

They were both skinny little things, their bony legs torn and bleeding as they dragged them across the concrete without a care. They pushed themselves up on their stick-like arms until they were standing, a full head shorter than Olivia and her mother. The girl closest to them turned to face them, the entire left side of her face clawed so badly it reminded Olivia of raw hamburger meat, her little eyeball hanging by a strand upon her ravaged cheek.

Miriam cried out as she threw her hand over her mouth. "Dear God!" she moaned and then gagged. She bent over and retched into the grassy yard without warning.

Olivia hesitated. She knew what she had to do, but the humanity in her screamed in opposition, rooting her where she stood. Her bat swirled through the air slightly behind her head as she readied herself. She would only do it in self-defense. She wouldn't attack innocent kids who are clearly hurt beyond repair. Maybe these people were crazed with their pain and didn't know what they were doing. But then the image of Maddie's fear-struck eyes pleading for help that Olivia couldn't provide flashed in her mind just as the two girls lunged forward.

Using her bat like a bo staff as Axel had showed her, she swung forward and cracked the first girl in the left temple then swung back and cracked the other in the right, felling them both in one instant. Unable to stop now, Olivia grabbed her mother by the arm and forced her forward with her.

"Axel's house is right there!" she shouted, dragging Miriam toward a white two-story house with black shutters across the street. "We can make it! Come on!"

Miriam swayed as she ran, her head spinning from being sick and the things she'd seen, but her feet kept moving. She stumbled over the curb at the end of the driveway and fell to her knees. Somehow she had dropped Jennifer's bat and had to push up with her hands as Olivia yanked on her upper arm.

"Come on, mom! Let's go! It's right there!"

They reached the door as more mangled bodies came out of the woodwork, appearing from behind houses and vacant open doorways. Olivia banged her fist on the slick black door to Axel's house, her knuckles splitting and leaving little splatters of blood.

"Axel, it's Olivia, open up, please!" she cried out as loud as she could. She knew the sound would only draw more of these people to them, but it was also their only possible salvation from this hell on earth.

She screamed as three shuffling forms made their way slowly up the driveway, stumbling over the same lip Miriam had but righting themselves in their molasses movements. "Axel, come on!" Olivia screamed with all her might. "OPEN UP!"

The front door was thrown open, Axel standing dumbfounded in his black basketball shorts and t-shirt, his blue Mohawk askew as if he'd just woken up. Without a word of explanation Olivia thrust her mother through the doorway and followed after, closing them inside and twisting every lock she could find. Her chest rose and fell heavy as the thuds of banging fists erupted.

"What is going—" Axel started to say but Olivia threw herself at him, wrapping her arms tightly around his neck, pressing her body against his until she felt they were one, and she burst into tears. She cried for Maddie and for Jennifer and all the nameless, sometimes faceless, people that roamed the street. Why was this happening? What had caused such a terrible catastrophe? She squeezed her eyes shut tight and prayed it was all a nightmare as Axel cradled the back of her head in his hands, petting her long straight hair in an attempt to calm her. She tried to compose herself but it was useless. Could she have done anything differently to save her friends from the fate they met? How could she just leave their bodies there to be ravaged by these monsters? But what choice did she really have? If she had tried to get any closer she would have ended up just like them.

"Olivia?" Axel spoke softly, tears gathering in his eyes from sheer sympathy since he had no idea what was happening in the world outside his front door.

Olivia peeled herself from Axel and stood hunched over, her head hung low as the tears continued to fall. "Maddie and Jennifer," she sobbed as she wiped at her nose and eyes. "They're dead."

"What? What do you mean they're—"

"They're dead!" she shouted, not because she was angry with him but with herself. "The world has gone to shit! People are eating each other out there! And I couldn't save them…" she spoke this last part in almost a whisper. "I couldn't save them."

VI

As the seconds ticked by, the banging on the door grew louder. Axel, unable to contain his curiosity for the new world, pulled the curtain to the front picture window aside the tiniest bit and peered through. It was definitely people, human beings, trying to beat their way into the house, though their movements were not like those of someone trying to get it. Their arms moved as if they carried massive weight, slow and lagging as they lifted them and tossed them into the door. Randomly and all over their body Axel took note of the various size and severity of wounds that all seemed to carry. The woman with a short dark bob who was in the front of the small army was missing a chunk out of her arm but barely seemed to acknowledge it as she continued her half-efforts to get in. The man next to her was covered in scratches that penetrated down to his bones, his flesh hanging in ragged loose ribbons that waved in the summer breeze.

Axel groaned from the sickness that rose from the depths of his stomach and he backed away, letting the curtain fall to conceal them once more. "So, what do we do?" he asked, more to himself than the two terrified women in the room. He was used to thinking on his toes and taking charge in high-intensity situations. It was a big part of his martial arts training. "What do we do? What do we do?" he kept muttering to his feet as he paced the living room floor.

"We can't stay here," Olivia said with finality, having cried all the tears her body could produce.

"Why not? We could make this place safe, find ways to board the doors, the windows. We could stay here."

As if in confirmation of what Olivia said, a large head came crashing through the front window, showering the beige carpet in a sprinkle of glass. They all screamed and backed away as the man tried to force his way through the small hole his head had made. The jagged edges of the glass tore at the flesh of his bare arms as he scraped and pushed to make it bigger. With little effort, the glass complied and gave way, leaving a gaping entrance into their safe haven.

"Upstairs!" Axel yelled as he turned and ran, grabbing Miriam and Olivia by the arms, but Olivia dug her heels in.

"No!" she yelled and tugged her arm away from him. "If we go upstairs they'll just trap us again and we'll have nowhere to go. We have to get out of here. We can't stay."

"But if we—" he started to say but Olivia cut him off when she grabbed him by the shoulders forcefully.

"Axel, we can't stay here," her grip was determined though her voice had softened to a loving gentleness.

He stared into her eyes as the groans and beating continued only a few feet away. "OK. We can head out the garage. That'll give us a head start at least."

The front door lay a good twenty feet back from the garage's entrance. If they could use the side service door to escape they could make their way across the neighborhood unseen, at least by the mutants who were trying to get through the window. Who knew what else was lurking around the house. For all they knew they were surrounded.

Olivia grabbed Axel's hand in hers and took Miriam's in her other. Together, they left the living room, crept down the hallway, and reached the garage door off the kitchen. There was a loud crash from the front that made them all jump in panic. The window had held up as long as it could but there were just too many for it to withstand. It came crashing down as bodies fell to the floor in a heap, one on top of another. They moaned and struggled to get their bearings to stand as more bodies writhed beneath them.

Axel thrust open the door and motioned for Miriam and Olivia to go quietly. He closed the door behind him with delicacy, peeking through the crack to see one of the mangled bodies lunge around the corner of the hallway. The three walked on eggshells, their legs burning from the effort to be soundless. He opened the side service door slowly and quietly, peering his head out to check for safety. The side yard was clear. There wasn't a soul around to witness them in their escape.

Olivia was the first to step back outside and into the summer sunshine. If crazed, murderous cannibals weren't trying to get them this actually would have been a really nice day. Her team would have won their game. Out of state college scouts would have surrounded her, wanting her information so they could persuade her to attend their school, far away from this place. Whatever was happening, was it happening everywhere or was this some alien isolated incidence? She wished they'd had time to turn on the news, even for a few moments, just to hear what was really going on. Someone, somewhere had to know what was going on!

They all grasped hands again and Axel led them past the garage and down the driveway. None of the people who had been beating on the door were there any longer. They were all in the house sniffing out the lost scent of living flesh, the fresh dinner that was tiptoeing softly away on uncut grass. It wasn't until they crossed the street and headed through another neighbor's yard that Olivia realized the direction they were going. She tugged back on her boyfriend's arm desperately.

"We can't go that way," she said pleadingly.

Axel stopped though she could tell his body didn't want to. "Why not?"

The last reserve of tears Olivia thought she'd already expended collected in the corners of her eyes. "Because Maddie is there. I can't face her. I can't see what they've done —" she took a ragged breath.

Axel brought her hand to his lips and kissed it to calm her. "OK. We'll go…" he took a second to scan the area for potential threats, "…this way." He pointed north. Olivia and Miriam followed without question.

They snuck between the houses in what was once a quiet suburban neighborhood. Now it rang with the horrific sounds of screams and moans and death. They almost made it out without meeting another crazed citizen, making it to highway twelve which they could then cross and head into the woods of the Dunes State Park. Olivia knew that was the plan the moment Axel had signaled north. It made sense that's where he would think to go. It was only last night they had been there sledding down the sand dunes. She remembered the shadowed figure she'd seen at the top of the dune before she ever ventured to climb it and the foreboding feeling it gave her. Could it have been one of these sick people up there? Could they really have been that close to death even then? She pushed the thought from her mind before she was consumed in questions she'd never have answers to.

Olivia couldn't help noticing her mother's whimpering at the sight of one of the sick people, for that was the only explanation any of them could come up with for their depraved behavior. It pained her mother to see them so badly beaten, bruised, ravaged by teeth and claws of their own kind. It turned her stomach to imagine one of them reaching out and yanking away her only daughter before her eyes to devour her like they were some vengeful and scorned pagan God. She followed closely, but the longer they jogged and crept through the neighborhoods on the way to the Dunes State Park, the more space grew between her and her daughter.

Axel on the other hand never let Olivia's hand leave his. His fingers gripped her so tightly she was sure he would leave black and blue marks, but she didn't mind. The last thing she wanted was to be separated, to be left alone in this new and crazy world of inconsistent savagery. She kept her eyes ahead on her boyfriend's blue spiky mohawk as it swayed in the hot breeze. Sweat broke out on her forehead and under her arms. She thought about shedding her softball uniform for the t-shirt and shorts she wore underneath but then realized that the sun was sinking behind the horizon and it would soon be night. With the breeze off the lake it could still feel chilly without the sun to warm her bronzed cheeks. So she kept everything on and she kept moving forward into the unknown.

"Finally!" Olivia heaved when she saw the familiar sand dune rise before her. "You have no idea how happy I am to see you!" she said to the Devil's Slide.

"We're still not safe. We need to find some sort of shelter for the night and maybe gather some more supplies. I only have a few water bottles and snacks in the bag," Axel said, nodding to the black backpack resting on his shoulders. It was the one he took to every karate practice so there was very little in the way of survival in there; an extra pair of socks, a different t-shirt, a pair of boxer-briefs, three bottles of water, a package of beef jerky, a few protein bars, a small container of salted nuts that was half empty…nothing they could survive long on, but none of them really thought they would be out in the wilderness alone long trying to survive. And food was the last thing on any of their minds.

Surely someone would come to help the poor sufferers of Chesterton, Indiana. Surely there would be reinforcements coming to their aid soon. They can't just be left on their own. A shiver ran down Olivia's spine as she tried to convince herself all she thought then was true, but a little voice inside her was fighting it, whispering that this was it and soon she would be even more alone than she was now. Soon it would just be her and everyone she loved would become a ravenous cannibal like the people who murdered Maddie, like the one who ate Jennifer. Her stomach lurched and she bent over, breathing heavily as she stared at her shoes with her hands clutching her knees.

"Are you OK?" Axel asked with a gentle hand on her back.

"Sweetie?" her mother inquired softly. "Grab her some water," she ordered Axel.

He complied, tossing off his backpack and digging through it. "It's a little warm, but it'll do."

Olivia waved it off and attempted to stand upright again. "I'm fine. Really. Let's keep going."

"Where are we going?" Miriam asked. There was no bite in her voice as there had been the night before when she met Axel. Only fear.

Olivia tuned out the voices around her as her boyfriend and mother discussed their plan. Her eyes were focused on the top of the dune in the tree line that seemed to kiss the darkening sky. That was where she'd seen it. At the time she'd been confused but now she saw it with such perfect clarity. It was one of those people, the sick ones, the murderous ones. She'd thought it was some kind of wild animal last night, but there was no mistaking it now. It had been one of them, just mere feet away…and she'd said nothing. She'd told no one about it. She'd brushed it off as nothing and continued on with the playfulness of the night like a naïve child.

Tears collected in Olivia's eyes and spilled over the brim of her big brown eyes.

"Honey, what's wrong?" her mother fussed, putting both her hands around her shoulder and shaking her a little.

Olivia wiped the tears with the back of her hands and tried to sniff them down into containment. "I saw one…up there," she said between heavy breaths, "last night. I told myself it was just an animal but it wasn't. It was one of them. It was one of them and I didn't say anything to anyone."

A thickness settled in the air around the three of them as they absorbed Olivia's heavy words.

"I said nothing and now Maddie and Jennifer are dead. They died a terrible, horrible, excruciating death. They were eaten alive, torn apart because of me!" By the end she was screaming, her voice echoing through the crevasses of the dunes and hills.

"Oh, honey," Miriam said uselessly, clutching her daughter closer but not knowing what else to say.

"This is not your fault," Axel said assuredly, his voice firm and finite. "You had no way of knowing what it was. Even if you had recognized it as a person, why would you think it was someone who was going to kill someone else? This is not your fault," he said again for good measure, hoping he had reached the depths of his girlfriend's guilt that he knew weighed heavily on her gentle heart. But he could see that she was lost in it, her tears now uncontrollable.

Axel reached out and took both of Olivia's hands in his own and gently pulled her toward him, out of her mother's frantic grasp. He looked down at her and put a finger under her chin to tilt her gaze up to his when he realized she didn't have it in her to meet his eyes on her own. "You are a good person, Olivia Darling. The best. And this is not your fault."

She huffed out a breakthrough of hopeful laughter as more tears squeezed from her eyes. He wiped at them with his thumbs, holding her face in his hands before he touched his lips to hers softly and kissed her. He didn't care if Miriam was watching or what she thought of him or them or anything really. All he wanted in that moment was take Olivia's pain away and make her see herself the way he saw her; as this unstoppable, courageous, wondrous young woman. "We're going to get through this…together. I promise I won't let anything happen to you," he said softly to her, his warm breath tickling the tip of her nose. "To either of you," he said a little louder to include Miriam.

The middle-aged woman brushed her sweaty hair from her forehead and smiled back in silent acceptance and appreciation. The lapping of the small waves on the lakefront further down the sandy hill was all they heard as they stood to gather their wits and strength. No one noticed the soft shuffling of feet drawing nearer to their turned backs. It was the hissing gurgling growl before the attack that warned them of the danger a mere seven feet away. Without hesitation Axel pushed Olivia from him and into Miriam, who was slightly further away. He raised his hands to guard his face and kicked out his right leg with all its might, sending the bloodied form backwards and to the ground.

It writhed, rolling back and forth to right itself lazily, emitting guttural growls from deep within its throat all the while.

"Let's get out of here!" Miriam screeched as she took Olivia's arm and tugged at her.

"Wait," Axel said, looking into Olivia's eyes. They exchanged thoughts with the slight shifts in the muscles of their faces. They both knew what had to be done if they wanted to remain safe.

Olivia reached out and handed Axel her bat, unable to do it herself. The thing on the ground was almost unrecognizable. She thought it was probably a woman with how short it was, but it could have been a young teen boy. Its hair was cut short, large chunks missing as if it'd been ripped from the scalp with brutal force. Bloody, tender, ragged skin hung where locks should have been. Its face had been bitten, chewed, clawed, and devoured to the point of no return. Both cheeks were missing and Olivia could see right through to the teeth inside its mouth. Its t-shirt and jeans were torn to shreds that hung loosely on its body, saturated in its own black blood. One of its arms hung lower than the other, the opposite shoulder jutting upward making it move in a lopsided manner.

With much effort, it finally gained its bearings and pushed itself up to its feet again. Axel took the bat and gave a solemn nod to the other two before turning back around. He walked slowly up to the creature, for that was all it was to him now, all he could see it as if he was going to do what he was about to do. He couldn't think of it as a human being, someone like him with hopes and dreams, a past and no more future. It was an it, a thing, a monster, and it had to be stopped.

With a crack that reverberated through his entire body, Axel smashed the side of the thing's head in at the temple with the blunt piece of wood he gripped with pure white fingers. Instantly, the being crumpled to the ground in a sad heap of disfigurement.

Olivia stepped forward to join Axel at his side despite her mother pawing at her arm to keep her near her. Miriam groaned and crept forward cautiously to stand behind the other two. Axel stared down at the yellowing eyes stunned wide-open. The jaw hung to the side as if it had been dislocated in the blow. The teeth were stained red with blood. Whether it was its own or someone else's, no one wanted to think about it. Axel tried to swallow but his throat was as dry as the sand dunes around them.

"Let's find somewhere to camp for the night. We'll try to find help in the morning."

"Shouldn't we keep looking for help now?" Miriam said with new panic rising in her voice as the sun set behind the horizon, reflecting off the undulating lake in pinks and oranges and blues. "Shouldn't we try to find someone who can tell us what's going on and give us a place to stay that's safer than this? Why did you bring us out into the middle of nowhere anyway? Why did we listen to you? We're going to be eaten in our sleep if we stay here!"

Olivia walked straight up to her mother and slapped her across the cheek with all the force she could muster. Immediately, a red handprint emerged from the woman's pasty white skin. She raised her hand as if to confirm that it had actually happened.

"Sorry, mom, but you were getting hysterical."

Her mother's eyes narrowed into slits as she evaluated her daughter and the motives that lie beneath the assault to her face. "I'm not hysterical. I'm practical. It makes absolutely no sense to leave shelter to wander out in the middle of the woods with no protection while there are murderous crazy people eating each other out here!"

"It does make sense," Axel said calmly. He didn't want to feed the fire that was growing between Olivia and her mother at that moment, but he wanted both to understand his decision to bring them there. "In the house we were confined, trapped, and they were getting in. Just like they would any house they set their sights on. We would keep backing ourselves into a corner in the house until we were trapped with no way out and then they would take us. But out here we are open. We have options. We have the advantage of the tall dunes to look down and assess what's going on around us. We have the lake on one side, meaning we are not surrounded on all four sides. We can swim right out into it if we have to escape. There are trees to climb and hide in, small buildings to rest in temporarily that have windows on all sides so we can see if any of them are coming. I brought us here because it *is* our best chance at survival until someone saves us."

"If anyone saves us," Miriam spoke the words they had all been thinking.

"Of course someone will save us," Axel said as if he didn't have doubt overtaking his every thought. "They have to. There's the Army, the National Guard, the Coast Guard, the government, FEMA, *someone*. This is an epic disaster and we're not going to be left to fend for ourselves indefinitely. They don't do that to hurricane victims, tornado victims, or any other natural disaster victim. Why would they do that to us?" The question was rhetorical, and a good thing because Olivia and

Miriam avoided his eyes and looked at their shoes with no reply on their tongues.

Axel nodded his head once as if in satisfaction. "This way," he said, walking around the Devil's Slide to a small wooden bridge over the marsh.

VII

With the night there was an onslaught of noises in the woods no one in the group was used to. Olivia had expected it to be dead silent so they could effectively listen for any of the diseased sneaking up on them but there were so many critters and deer walking around that it was impossible. Once they were consumed in the dense blackness of night, Olivia's eyes adjusted best they could. She walked forward with large steps to avoid any raised roots hoping to trip her. Sometimes her mind got the best of her and when she stumbled over a branch she imagined it was the hand of someone on the ground reaching up to pull her down and devour her. Whenever this happened she would clutch her bat so tightly her hands ached and her breathing became shallow and rapid. Axel and her mother said nothing even though she was sure they had to hear the difference in her in those moments. She assumed nothing was said because they too experienced the same uncontrollable fear.

"I was sure the bird sanctuary building or information building or whatever was right up here this way," Axel said after an hour of walking in what he hoped wasn't circles in the dark.

"Even if it was we wouldn't see it," Miriam said softly, just above a whisper. "I can't see anything." As if in confirmation, she banged her knee against something solid and hard. With caution she reached her hand down until she felt the offending object. She ran her hands across its smooth flat surface. "I think I found a bench!" she said with glee, though she wasn't sure why this should excite her. Maybe it was the sense of familiarity a bench brought her. Benches were a symbol of civilization, a reminder of the way life was yesterday.

"We must be really close then," Axel said, an added note of chipper in his muted voice.

Olivia stopped in the middle of what she assumed was one of the dirt trails that wound through the acres of State Park woods. She tilted her head up to the sky. Between the swaying leaves of the towering trees she spotted little balls of white lights twinkling. She turned and searched for the moon as the summer wind rustled her hair against her back. In that moment of peace she didn't realize the other two had walked ahead without her. From a distance she heard the joyous whisper call of her boyfriend. "Here it is! We found it!"

"Yes!" her mother exhaled. Olivia followed the sound of her exultation to catch up to them. "Now let's hope it's unlocked."

"Depending on who was here and what happened, it just might be," Axel said, reaching out to take hold of the handle. He paused before pulling to inhale a deep breath. He held it in as he gave the door a good yank. It opened swiftly, throwing him back and almost off his feet because half his heart had been expecting it to be locked.

"Ladies first," he said, holding the door open and ushering his girlfriend and her mother in, though he followed closely behind. The second the door shut he turned the lock. It was of little comfort seeing as almost the entire building was windows that looked out into the entrance to the park's trails, the seemingly endless wooded area that had in the blink of an eye become their only home.

"What now?" Olivia asked, finally lowering her bat from a ready stance and taking a look around, though it was too dark still to see anything. She thought about turning on the lights and then decided against it. It would be a homing beacon for the monstrous people out there to find them. Darkness was scary, uncertain, and unfamiliar, but it also meant safety in this instance.

"I know what I'm going to do," Miriam said as she walked deeper into the building and crossed behind the desk. "And that's have some much needed privacy in the bathroom."

"Uhg, mom!" Olivia groaned though there was a hint of laughter beneath.

"Everyone does it," her mother chuckled as she disappeared behind a door. "Remember the book I got you when you were little!"

"Yeah, yeah, just go," her daughter laughed and then turned to her boyfriend. As if they had been waiting with bated breath for a moment alone together, Axel and Olivia fell into each other's arms and held tightly to one another. It was as if they couldn't get close enough, though there was none of the sexual tension that had plagued them days before. They found security in the familiar touch of each other, a familiarity that allowed them to breathe in peace for just a moment.

"What are we going to do now?" Olivia heaved into his warm neck. She was on the verge of tears but decidedly kept them at bay. She'd cried enough for a lifetime on that day alone.

"I wish I had all the answers, sweetie, but I don't. I don't know what to do next except try to sleep and see how things are in the morning."

"Maybe we'll wake up and this will all have been a bad dream," Olivia said half-jokingly.

Axel rested a hand on the back of her head and pet at her silky long hair, his cheek on her forehead. "Maybe, pumpkin. Maybe." They broke apart when Miriam came back ten minutes later.

"I'm going to clear the place, make sure there's nothing surprising lurking anywhere," Axel said, taking Miriam's bat from her. "Stay here and keep an eye out until I return.

"Will do," Olivia said, raising her bat up as if to show she was ready for anything again.

He disappeared around the corner into an adjacent room that was meant for seminars and nature classes in the summer months. Olivia heaved a breath and shuffled over to the wall across from the bird lookout wall of windows. There were rows and rows of tanks housing a variety of creepy crawlies; snakes, spiders, bugs, and some seemingly empty that she hoped the things were only hiding and hadn't escaped.

When Axel returned with the good news that he hadn't met anyone else in his search inside or outside the building they were able to release the tension they'd been carrying in their shoulders. They piled their bats and backpack together, sat down behind the front desk for concealment. Miriam sat up against the wall, one leg bent up to rest her arm and head on while the other lay limply extended out. Axel followed suit but encouraged Olivia to try to lay down, her head cradled in his lap as he stroked her tresses gently. No one made the plan to stay awake, to keep watch and take turns. They were each too exhausted to keep their eyes open a minute longer. In the quiet of the night they fell asleep and remained asleep until the first rays of dawn shone through the thick glass windows again.

Days came and went in much the same way for Olivia, Axel, and Miriam. They ventured out in the mornings looking for food, supplies, people, anything they could find. Almost always they happened upon another out-of-their-mind being moving languidly toward them, their mouths masticating before ever tasting their tender flesh, ready to rip it apart the moment it touched their blood-stained lips. But no one in the small group was ever caught. Each in their own way became comfortable in defending themselves against these monsters with their weapons. With nearby stores and restaurants they gathered a small arsenal to choose from, which they kept hidden in the observation building, their new temporary home base. They had butcher knives, kitchen knives, even a Samurai sword Axel had taken from the wall of a nearby sushi joint. He used it with great precision, having trained with something similar in his karate classes. He was the deadliest of them all and was always the first to run toward the danger to protect the one thing left he had that he loved. He was even starting to like her mother, too.

Despite their searching, they hardly came across another human being like them, someone desperate for safety and normalcy, someone not foaming red at the mouth for the taste of human flesh. It was quiet. It was eerie. It was surreal when they stepped onto highway twelve and didn't encounter a single car in passing. That's when they realized this was not going to be a short-lived thing. This was their new reality and all they had was each other. Once the idea was concrete within them they defended each other with new loving ferocity like never before. People or not, who knew what they were anymore. All they knew was that they were not going to let one of those monsters take any of them down.

The sun was shining high above the trees. It'd been almost a week since the group of three took shelter in the State Park observation building. In that time they'd learned a lot about their new world. They learned that whatever was happening to the people it was degenerative. They were rotting away but somehow still walking around. They were losing limbs, blasted with guns in the stomach, entrails dragging behind them, and nothing slowed them down unless the brain was damaged beyond repair. It was as if they felt no pain, no fear, as if they were oblivious to life itself.

The second thing they learned was that it spread like a disease. The way they discovered this haunted Olivia's nightmares. In one of their daily searches they came across a young couple trapped in their vehicle that had crashed into a tree. One female, the passenger it seemed since she jumped out of that side of the car, reached back in for the other female. She cried desperately for the driver to just take her hand but Olivia could tell by the piercing cries that it was too late. The driver's door was wide open and the satisfying groans of the dead-like people ripping and tearing and eating at her flesh was all too familiar now. The woman on the outside of the car had tears streaming down her face.

"We should help them," Olivia wanted to whisper desperately but her mouth remained shut. She knew beyond a doubt that it was too late to help anyone as the larger woman with short salt and pepper hair took off down the road on foot as fast as her swollen feet could carry her. There was really no need. The diseased had their hands full with mouth-watering distraction anyway.

Before long the large woman had gotten away and the desperate cries of pain within the car had subsided. Olivia turned in her squat, sneaking out of sight of what was going on, concealed by the trees and bushes of the woods, but Axel reached out and grabbed her wrist to still her.

"Wait," he said.

"There's nothing we can do. We should get out of here before they turn on us."

Miriam nodded her head vigorously in agreement. "I'm with Liv on this one. There's too many and they'll be finished with that poor woman soon." She bit her lip after she spoke, wondering when sentences like that became normal practice. No matter how many people she saw eaten, torn apart, murdered cold-blooded before her eyes, it never ceased to turn her stomach.

"I have a theory and I want it proven," was all Axel gave them as he sat in wait.

Silence overtook the gruesome scene as the woman was drained of her blood. The inside of the car looked like the worst crime scene imaginable with blood splattered thickly on all the windows, from the front to the back.

"What are we waiting for?" Olivia asked, unable to hide the irritation in her voice. They were supposed to be on their way to find more food and water, which they were running dangerously low on. It was pointless to sit and waste time watching someone who was beyond help, until it wasn't.

Before their eyes, the woman from the car snarled and growled, swiping at the others around her. Immediately, the gathering backed away and shuffled off into the surrounding woods. The woman pulled herself out of the car warily and stood on wobbly legs.

"Shut up," Olivia blurted out. "There's no way that woman is alive."

"That's what I suspect, too," Axel said to her surprise. "I think she's one of them now."

"One of them? So what, we are trapped inside a zombie apocalypse or something? That's insane. These people are drugged or sick or something like that. There's no way they are the walking dead. That's impossible," Olivia rambled off, trying to convince herself that what she said was true rather than Axel's theory.

Slowly she tapered off and watched the woman, with her long black hair now knotted and matted with blood, follow the others off into the woods to find her first meal.

"Well, that confirms it," Axel said. "Now let's go get some more supplies."

VIII

Days dragged on as they lie in wait for someone, anyone, to rescue them from their living nightmare. No one came. The last living people they encountered were the women in the car, and who knew where the one who escaped ran off to or if she was even still alive. All they saw was the undead, piles and piles of them, walking in hordes in search of something to quench their never-ending thirst for blood and hunger for human flesh. Several times Olivia, Axel, and Miriam had to defend themselves against these things. Axel always rushed forward while Olivia and Miriam took care of anything that got past him, though they rarely did. Axel was quick with his sword, almost always felling the savage beasts with one quick stroke. His blade was sharp but his reflexes were sharper, ever more so since put to constant use in this new reality.

Often Olivia found herself watching Axel slash open these used-to-be people, blood splattering his ivory complexion to mix with the many faint freckles on his skin. She watched as the muscles of his arms loosened and contracted with great strength in wielding his weapon of choice, his body scarcely covered most days as he walked around shirtless in his gym shorts trying not to overheat. She watched his tattoos dance on his skin as the muscles beneath rippled with effort. What was wrong with her? How could she feel anything but deep seeded disgust at what was happening? How could she be filled with desire in moments like these? Whether she wanted to feel or not, seeing Axel charge forward with his sword and take down their enemies with precision made her want to shove him to the ground and kiss him hard, pressing her body against his solid muscles in passion. The only thing refraining her from doing so was common sense and the presence of her mother, hand always covering her mouth in fear for the boy she used to despise.

On this particular day the sun shone high in the sky with a heat that radiated off the burnt skin of the survivors. Though it had only been a little over a week of walking the woods and scavenging abandoned stores and homes for supplies their demeanor relaxed. They walked a little slower, they held their weapons a little softer, and they talked a little louder. Olivia and Miriam laughed together as they listened to Axel's stories about some of the funny mishaps he'd encountered in his martial arts class, especially the ones involving the big hulking Brant. Those made Olivia laugh the hardest. Miriam didn't get why they were so funny because she had never met the lumbering oaf. Olivia wondered if all his brain had kept him alive.

"Much of it was discipline, but the occasional shenanigans still went on," Axel laughed with them. "How about you Mrs. D," he asked casually. "Got any funny stories?"

At this Miriam faltered, her face slackening with a flood of memories. Olivia nudged Axel and widened her eyes in reprimand. Miriam swallowed and then shook her head. "No, it's OK, sweetie. I just…it just kills me not knowing what happened to your father. I know we didn't always seem to get along. Life got in the way and I became so busy."

Miriam stopped, her hands on her hips and her face turned up toward the summer sun. She basked in it with closed eyes as she pictured her husband's round, scruffy face. "Between work and keeping up with the house I became too busy for fun. I didn't know how to loosen up and enjoy my family anymore because I viewed everything in life as a chore…even you and your father," she said turning to her daughter and taking her hand. "I'm so sorry I didn't spend more time with the both of you. I'm sorry I worked so hard for money and not nearly hard enough for your love, for your father's love. It'd been so long since we held each other…kissed…and now I'll probably never…" she said through the tears that pooled in her eyes.

Olivia couldn't help herself. She let the wetness flow down her face as she assured her mother it was OK. For years she'd resented her and how much she worked, how little time she spent with Olivia or even acknowledged her existence. All along her mother thought she was doing right by her family and Olivia never looked at it that way. She always thought work was the escape from the family that wasn't good enough, but that wasn't it at all. She had been working *for them*. Olivia threw her arms around her mother's neck and hugged her tightly. They wept silently together, drowning in their forgiveness of one another for the years of neglect and resentment unspoken.

Axel stood back, resting against a tree with his arms crossed, his sword leaning against the trunk as he watched the beautiful sight before him. It made him think of his own parents. They weren't home when the apocalypse hit. Both his mother and father worked in a laboratory in downtown Chicago, his father a geneticist and his mother a lab assistant. Both were far away when the dead came back to devour their town. He had no idea if Chicago was dealing with the same thing or not, but since no one had come to aid the little lakeside town of Chesterton, Indiana he assumed the zombies had consumed everything. Surely their disease was spreading across the homefront. More and more crossed their paths every day but it was easy to defeat them now. One blow to the head with the bat or a slice with the sword and they were down for good. He could hear them coming from a mile away because of the dragging of their lazy feet, the snapping of twigs, the thudding of their bodies hitting the ground when the inevitably tripped over a root sticking up out of the ground. They weren't the most coordinated of beings and for that he was grateful.

But Axel was jerked from his thoughts by an ear-splitting shriek.

"LOOK OUT!" his girlfriend shouted as she pointed at him.

His entire body tensed as he jumped away from the tree, sword in hand and at the ready just behind his head. The shambling living corpse had missed grabbing him by milliseconds. Its fingers clawed at the tree where Axel had just been, its mouth watering with insatiable hunger, its teeth dripping with fresh dark blood.

There was another scream from Miriam as she held onto Olivia tight. Axel turned, a full three-sixty this time, and suddenly realized the grave situation they were in. They were surrounded on all sides, zombies closing in faster than he could possibly take them down. Without pausing to think, he swung his sword through the temple of the decrepit man that had tried to grab him. That was one down…only about twenty more to go. A small voice in his head warned him that this was it. This was the end of the line. He resolved that if that was true they would at least go down swinging.

Olivia followed suit, breaking free from her mother's grasp to swing her bat with full force. It cracked against the head of the next closest undead, a young woman with stringy black hair and glad her jaw missing. She crumpled to the ground but her limbs still stirred. Olivia let out the cry of a warrior and smashed the thing's head repeatedly with her bat until it was nothing more than an unrecognizable mess of blood and brains.

Miriam gripped her bat and tried swinging it, but she missed contact, hitting the thing in the shoulder instead. The large man in overalls and dingy tank top stumbled backwards, as if caught off guard, but then pushed forward again. He grabbed Miriam's arm in his cold, tough hands and she dropped her weapon. It rolled across the ground getting kicked about in the stir and chaos.

"RUN!" she shouted to Olivia, her eyes locking with her daughter's.

"Mom!" Olivia yelled and ran the few steps to her aid but the robust male swung his free arm through the air manically. Olivia leaned back to avoid being gouged by his blackened broken nails.

"RUN!" Miriam shouted again, this time to both Olivia and Axel. More bodies shuffled over, drawn by the commotion and the promise of a fresh, tender meal. Miriam kept pushing the man's head away, somehow avoiding his large teeth in all the confusion, but she knew she couldn't keep it up for long. "I want you to run!" she commanded over her shoulder, surprisingly firm and calm.

"I'm not leaving you," Olivia shrieked as the others ignored her and Axel to head for the now growing horde around her mother.

"You have to," Miriam started to say but ended up screaming in anguish by the end. The man had finally achieved his goal and sunk his teeth into the tender flesh of her arm.

"NO!" Olivia cried, tears overflowing as she sank to her knees. There was nothing she could do. Even if she braved the horde and tried to save her mom they all knew her mother would turn in the end. They'd seen it before. Miriam was as good as one of them, but that knowledge didn't make listening to her demise any easier. It tore Olivia's heart in two to hear the cries.

"I love you," Miriam struggled to say, her eyes trained on Olivia's as if they were all she could see.

By then Axel had grabbed Olivia by the shoulders and was ready to turn her to lead her away to safety. But Olivia fought his force, wrenching her shoulders from his grip for one last look at her mother. "I love you, mom. I always have and always will."

"Take...care...of her," Miriam choked the order to Axel as the horde closed in and fell on her, dragging her to the ground with them in a tangled mess of decaying flesh.

"Mom!" Olivia sobbed, her bat lying useless on the ground next to her.

Axel picked her up, setting her on her feet to make their escape while the horde was still distracted. By then the anguished cries had subsided and he knew there was little time left to make their escape. He all but had to carry her and all the weapons, dragging Olivia every inch of the way away from where her mother had just stood hugging her. Tears flowed freely down Axel's face though a sound never escaped his stern-set lips. He hadn't answered Miriam in that moment, but their eyes had made the unbreakable promise. He would take care of Olivia, he would keep her alive no matter what, and he would not let Miriam down.

IX

The two only made it as far as the safety of their shelter, which they hadn't been that far from when the horde descended upon them. They shut themselves behind the glass doors and crumpled to the floor together behind the front desk. Olivia sobbed uncontrollably, hiding her face in Axel's chest.

She heaved so hard he was afraid she would drown in her own tears if she didn't stop to catch her breath.

In the morning Olivia's eyes were so swollen from an entire night of crying that she could hardly see from them. She rubbed them with the back of her hands as she righted herself from Axel's lap but that only made them sting, which reminded her of why they were so sore in the first place. Her lip started to quiver but then she took a deep breath and resolved to remain stoic, like her mom had been all her life. There was nothing left inside Olivia anyway.

Axel felt her stir and immediately sat up with her. "Hey," he said in a gruff morning voice. He stretched high over his head, his back cracking in relief.

"Morning," Olivia answered weakly.

Heavy silence settled in as Olivia's mind wandered, trying desperately to not recall the sight of the zombies falling on her mother to devour her. All the while Axel assessed her and her mental state.

"I think maybe we should pack up and move on from here," he concluded when he saw her using everything she had left inside to contain the tears that still wanted to flow from her beautiful eyes.

This distracted her from her thoughts. She turned to him with her brows furrowed in confusion.

"Yeah, I just think maybe we have overstayed our welcome. We're going to run out of resources in this area if we keep picking it over. And who knows, maybe the wandering dead will get wise to where we are staying. I have no idea how it all works still," he said, starting to ramble. He went silent when he saw Olivia had not moved a muscle in her expression as she listened. With a deep breath to clear his rant, he started again. "We might even be able to find a house," he ventured, taking her hands in his and holding them to his chest. "One that's fortified or that we can refortify. We can make a home in this mess for ourselves."

Olivia's muscles relaxed and her face softened as she looked at the young man clutching her hands desperately to him. It had been weeks since they had the comforts of home. His once tall and spiky blue mohawk now hung down in strands at his broad and angular shoulders. Most days, like this one, he gathered it atop his head in a small bun to keep his neck cool. His skin was no longer a pale splatter of freckles but a warm bronze with the occasional red patch of burn. More often than not he wore his black gym shorts and nothing else, not wanting to overheat with the unreliability of clean water to drink. The backs of her fingers brushed against his hard chest, rising up and down with his deep, soft breaths. That stirring inside her rose again.

She smiled as much as her grief would allow her in the moment. "OK," she said softly.

"Yeah?" his voice rose along with his eyebrows. He brought her knuckles to his lips and kissed them over and over again.

They both released breathy laughs of mutual affection. When the joy of the moment had passed and the realization that they would soon be facing the unknown settled back in, Olivia made the decision not to waste what might be their last moments in the confines of actual shelter.

"Before we go," she said, holding his hands which were now rifling through the large backpack they had upgraded to on their last visit to the local Wal-Mart. He turned to her, his blue eyes radiating. "I want to," was all she said.

Axel sat there a moment like a statue, contemplating her riddle. As his ocean eyes searched her face for answers she looked up at him through her long dark lashes, fluttering them in half-embarrassment while she awaited his answer. Finally, realization hit and his lips parted, hung open in shock.

"Are you—are you sure? This would be your first...I mean, you've never…before….have you?" he stammered, his cheeks turning bright red.

Olivia's face followed suit. She felt her skin burn. "No," she said almost defensively, as if he were accusing her of being too prudish. But she was being silly and she knew it. She softened her voice as she stared down at her wringing hands. "I haven't. I didn't want to do it with just anybody. I saw how badly that turned out for some of my friends." Her reference to Jennifer sparked a flash of the moment she fell to her death, the sickened woman consuming her friend before her very eyes. She quickly dispelled the image with a few rapid blinks.

Whether it was right or not, fair or not, this was going to be her moment. It was still going to be special, even as the danger of being eaten alive by what were once her neighbors loomed just outside. "What I'm trying to say is last night made me realize we don't know what's going to happen to us from one moment to the next, and if I die tonight I want to die knowing I lived. And I'd want you to know without a doubt in your heart that I loved you…truly loved you while I lived."

Wetness collected in the corner of Axel's eyes. He cleared his throat and took her hand in his again, only this time he rubbed his thumb along the back sending pulsating sparks throughout her entire body. When he looked at her it was intensely and she almost got lost in the variations of blues in his eyes. She swore the colors undulated like the waves of the sea.

"You don't have to do that for me to feel that," he said with a small huff of laughter, as if that should have been obvious to her. When she realized he was about to reject her offer she quickly looked away so he wouldn't see the embarrassment burn into her face. "It's not that I don't want to," he said in a rush, scooching closer to her on the floor behind the reception desk where they sat. "I do. Believe me I do. But just because the world is falling apart around us doesn't mean civility has to, does it?"

"What's that supposed to mean?" She didn't want to sound offended but she could hear it come across in her voice.

Axel's lips upturned with a grin. "It means I think we have a good chance of finding a safe home to occupy if we really try. I know I spoke against it before but now, with what we've seen, I think it's possible. I can make it safe for you, bring you the comforts of a home, and there, in a bed, we can…show each other just how much we mean to one another. There, I would like to live as…" he faltered as Olivia sat on edge, leaning closer in anticipation of what he would say next. It was all so romantic she could barely take it. Here she was practically throwing herself at him and he had the decency to say 'Not here. Not like this'. It was so like Axel. The chaos of the fallen world had not changed him one bit. "I would like to live as husband and wife. I mean, I know we can't have a proper ceremony anymore and the sentiment might mean very little the way the world is right now, but—I don't know—it's how I was raised and it's a value I still hold dear in my heart and I don't want to let that go just because the world is crazy right now."

Olivia stared at him, processing what he said. Inside she was elated but her face was having trouble expressing it outwardly because she was so shocked such a man even existed at all.

The poor boy started to get nervous in her silence. "What do you think?" he asked, all confidence he'd previously owned flying right out the window. "I mean, I know you're only sixteen."

"Seventeen now, actually. If I'm counting my days right," she interrupted. Axel stared at her dumbfounded. "Your birthday," he said in anguish. "In all that's happened I totally forgot!"

"It's OK, really," Olivia laughed and pulled his hand from his face. "I think I can let it slide this once. But you better not forget another birthday or anniversary again."

At this his face brightened, splitting in two with an overjoyous grin. "It's like you said, we have no guarantee of the next day and if I'm going to die I want to die living to the fullest…as your husband." At that he straightened up again to his tall height, his shoulders back with confidence regained. "What do you say?"

Olivia couldn't help the laughter or the tears that flowed forth from her. Once she'd composed herself she was able to answer, "Let's do it."

"Yeah?" Axel asked with the biggest grin he'd ever displayed in his lifetime.

"Yeah."

He cupped Olivia's face in his large, slender hands and drew her to him, planting his lips delicately on hers. They both tasted tears as they silently celebrated their engagement. Axel broke away though it was the last thing in the world he wanted to do at that moment. His yearning for Olivia in mind, body, and soul was almost more than he could bear. He wanted her and every molecule in his body was on fire with that wanting. But he knew what they had to do. He turned back to his backpack and started taking inventory on what they had and what they needed.

"Looks like we have enough for at least two days here if we're conservative," he said, standing up. He reached out a hand to help Olivia to her feet. She brushed away the tears from her face with both hands and heaved a husky, breathy laugh.

"Sounds good," she agreed.

He nodded his head once as he maneuvered the backpack onto his shoulders. "Let's head out then."

It was still dark outside as the beginnings of the morning crept over the firm line of the horizon. The sky made its majestic transformation from dark blue to orange to pink to yellow and finally to a crisp bright light blue. For the entire day the two of them wandered the woods to get their bearings and come up with a plan for their safest course of action. Being by the lake definitely had its advantages, but it didn't seem to be the safest. The houses there had large windows and little reinforcements. Most of the houses were empty because the summer inhabitants had not made it out to open them back up for the season. No, getting away from the lake, the woods, and heading back into town was the best option.

"You know, though, it's funny how quickly your house with four solid walls and not much in the way of windows fell to the zombies but then we take up shelter in a building that is almost all windows and nothing happens," Olivia mused as they walked, her legs starting to ache from the constant movement.

"It is weird, but I think I know why. Out here in the woods there aren't many people and the zombies might know that. They walk through here and probably don't come across a single person for days so they move along lazily. But in a subdivision there are probably a lot of people all locked away in their houses. I'm not sure how much these zombies can think or know, but it sure seems like they know fresh flesh is around and they are almost in a frenzy to get at it," Axel reasoned away as Olivia hung on his wisdom.

"Makes sense," she agreed as she stepped over a fallen branch.

Hours crawled along as the hot summer sun blazed over the leafy trees sending rays dancing across their skin here and there.

"I need a break," Olivia huffed, as she doubled over with her hands on her waist trying to catch her breath. "And water."

Axel slung the bag onto the ground and rummaged through it. "Here you go," he said, handing her a mostly empty bottle.

She tipped it back and consumed every last wet drop before realizing she left nothing for Axel. She removed the bottle from her lips and handed it back to her boyfriend sheepishly. "Sorry," she said.

He brushed it off with a wave of his hand and packed up again. "No, don't worry. I wanted you to have it. We'll get more." He said this last bit so casually, as if they could stroll down to the quick mart on highway twelve and buy a case as people filled their cars with gas. In the normal world that would be how it would go. Not in the zombie world, though.

"Let's keep going for just a bit more," he urged her on. "We're close to the highway but not too close. We can stop in an hour and make camp for the night."

"You mean sleep outside?" Olivia asked with more fear in her voice than she would have liked.

"Well, yeah," Axel responded with a cock of his head. "What'd you think?"

"Honestly? I thought we'd be in a house by now eating pantry food and snuggling up under some covers. Who knew how big this park was anyway!"

Axel couldn't help laughing at this. "Very big. It's not just what you've seen in Chesterton but it goes all the way down to Michigan City and further. It's miles and miles of woods and dunes."

"OK. I'll sleep outside tonight. But tomorrow night we better be in a nice comfy bed and you better be rubbing my feet."

"Deal," he agreed whole-heartedly.

When night had finally fallen and there was only a small sliver of blue left in the almost black sky, the couple finally stopped and gave their tired feet a break. Axel searched through his bag for their impromptu dinner, handing Olivia a can of Spaghetti O's with chunks of hot dogs in it.

"Do you want me to make a small fire to heat those up for you?" he asked gallantly, to which Olivia quickly shook her head and let him off the hook.

"Oh no, cold dogs are fine with me. I'm not one of those high maintenance chicks." They both laughed quietly, more eager to devour what little food they had just then. "Man, I'm starving!" Olivia couldn't help expelling with the first bite. In less than a minute the entire can was gone. Axel sat there amazed, still gathering his own dinner. They sat closely together with nothing more than a small pocket flashlight on the ground to illuminate the curves of their faces to each other.

"You know," Axel started to say with his mouth full of cold baked beans. "I'm here for you if you need to talk."

Olivia set the empty can aside and wiped her hands on her legs, unsure of what else to do. "I know. Thank you. I just need some time."

A dozen responses to get her to open up ran through Axel's head but he chose to nod in complacency instead. Maybe time was all she needed. Time and the chance to process the horrific loss of her mother, who was really truly only a mother to her in the ways Olivia needed her to be in those very last moments of life.

The sudden snap of a twig sent both of them to their feet. Axel's sword lay at his feet and he snatched it up as he rose. The natural response was to call out to ask who was there but both kept their lips tightly pursed, not daring to move, even breathe, aside from their sidelong glances to each other.

From the shadows three large bodies shuffled out toward them. Axel's grip tightened on his sword and Olivia finally stooped to grab hold of her trusty bat. Her mother's bat. The one that had saved their lives countless times in the last weeks but couldn't save Miriam when Olivia needed it to most. In the darkness it was impossible to see any definition to what approached them; they were living shadows. It wasn't until they heard a soft chuckle that Olivia and Axel exchanged confused glances, their grips loosening on their weapons minutely.

"What do we have here?" the man in the middle said with a husky, deep voice. As he stepped into the small rays of light given off by the flashlight it was clear, without a doubt, they were dealing with three living, breathing people and not the rotting, shambling corpses of late.

Olivia lowered her bat but noticed that Axel kept his sword raised and at the ready. "Gentlemen," he said almost formally.

It was strange. Olivia knew that Axel was different from most people, almost vintage in his moral compass and speaking, but she had never heard him call anyone a gentleman before. Her bat remained lowered but she kept her grip firm, just in case.

"Looks like a couple-a young pups, John Boy," the thinner, shorter man to the left said.

The one called John Boy stood a whole head taller than the men on either side of him and at least twice as wide. He wore dirtied denim overalls with one of the clasps unbuttoned and a long sleeve white shirt underneath despite the thick humidity in the air. Atop his large head sat a camo baseball hat that threw a black shadow across his face. For all Olivia knew there was nothing under that baseball cap's shadow but a blank slate of peach skin. All she saw was cloth hanging down to touch his chest, a face mask that had to have been from the flu pandemic. Everyone had been forced to wear masks or bandanas everywhere they went in an attempt to stop the spread of the virus. This made it really hard to define any of the men before them.

The other two were dressed similarly in jeans and long sleeve shirts, one black and one forest green. And they both wore baseball hats and bandanas that hid their features.

Suddenly, an uneasiness spread through Olivia's stomach and twisted it into knots. Something wasn't right here. She should feel elated at seeing other human beings who didn't want to rip her face off and eat it. She should feel immense relief at being found by people who could help her and Axel. But she didn't feel any of those things. What she felt was fear.

Olivia stood a little closer to Axel and threw her bat over her shoulder with one hand, casually so as not to cause any alarm in their new friends, but if she needed to swing it was already raised and ready to go.

"What's in the bag there, pup?" One man asked with a high laugh. John Boy simply stood there with his hands shoved deep in his pockets, awaiting Axel's response.

"I don't know what this is, but I think it's time you turn around and go," Axel said, his voice firm. It wasn't nearly as deep as John Boy's and only half as intimidating, but there was a certainty behind it that couldn't be denied. Axel was not going to let them near either of them or their supplies. He was standing up for himself against three large bullies. It was what he had trained for all those years. He was a black belt for goodness sake. There was no fear in his piercing blue eyes as he stared directly at where the eyes of the three men should have been beneath their shadowy veil.

The men didn't turn and leave. In fact, they didn't budge an inch. The two men on either side laughed while John Boy leaned back casually, knowingly.

"OK," he said as if there was nothing more to do about it. John Boy turned his head to look at one companion and then the other. "Let's get 'em."

Axel's body wanted to tense up but he kept it calm with his sword raised and his eyes trained on the three men, wondering who would be the first to make a move but none did. They stood there with their hands in their pockets, huffs of laughter escaping from beneath their face masks. That's when Axel felt a white hot sting on the wrist of his sword hand causing him to drop it. Before he knew what happened someone had him in a bear hug from behind.

Olivia screamed as someone jumped out of the darkness behind her and grabbed her too. They pried the bat from her fingers and threw it far enough away that she wouldn't be able to get it if she somehow escaped their grip. It was unlikely. She felt her ribs crack as the man squeezed her like a boa constrictor.

"Now, yer gonna give us everything you have; your food, your supplies, your weapons. Yer gonna just hand 'em over and *maybe* we'll let you live." John Boy's voice was scratchy like the thick reddish hairs that peeked out from the top of his mask that was pulled down to only cover his mouth and not his nose.

"You bastard!" Olivia shouted, though her voice was strained.

Axel struggled, trying to remember his training but all he could think of in that moment was the horrors that could befall Olivia. What if the men didn't plan on just taking their stuff. What if they hurt Olivia? Raped her? Took her? Killed her? He couldn't let anything happen to her. With as deep a breath as he could manage while being constricted, he tried to quiet his mind to focus.

"Whatcha got here?" The man to the left of John Boy asked. He was of medium height and build, a walking shadow in his dark jeans and black shirt. He could have been a ghost for all they knew. How many were there? It was hard to tell. The man bent down and picked up Olivia's bat, considering it, weighing it in his hands.

Olivia thrashed until her feet left the ground, kicking wildly. "Put that down!" she screamed. "Leave it alone! Don't touch it!"

"Ooo," the men all jeered as they looked at each other in amusement. "Looks like we got ourselves a feisty little one."

"I like 'em feisty."

"She's tough," the man holding her said comically. "Better watch out. She might just break free and getcha!"

Everyone laughed together, their deep voices echoing in the darkness. No one was there to hear them. No one was there to help.

"You know what?" the man holding the bat said as he smacked it lightly against his palm. "This is a nice bat. Maybe I'll keep it."

Olivia thought about spitting in the man's face. He was tauntingly close. She tried to free her arms to reach out to her bat but they were pinned down at her side. She struggled, groaned, and kicked, but to no avail.

"I think I should test it out first, though. You know, make sure it works and all."

Without warning, the man cracked the bat with both hands across Axel's face sending him to the ground with a sickening thud as the man holding him released him in perfect timing. This wasn't their first rodeo.

Olivia screamed and wailed at the top of her lungs, fighting harder than ever to escape the man's grasp as Axel lay motionless on the ground. "Axel! No! Axel! Get up!" she cried over and over.

The men around her laughed like hyenas as she felt the bile in her stomach rise to her throat. He couldn't be dead. Not like that. Not at their hands. This was not the plan. If everyone in the world died from these God forsaken zombies, she at least always would have Axel. That was the plan. Not this!

With a twitch of his arm, Axel groaned and writhed on the ground. Olivia stood motionless for a second and gave a heaving sigh of relief. "Axel!" she cried again.

Hearing her voice revived him to the situation they were in. He weakly pushed himself up on all fours. His head spun. It felt like it'd been split open, his bones turned to pulp in his face, his head pounding with a wrath unlike anything he'd ever felt before. But he pushed through it to stand on his feet. He pushed through it because he'd made a promise to Miriam he couldn't break.

"Take it!" Olivia shouted to the men as he saw them laughing at Axel's determination. "Take it all. We don't care! Just leave us alone!"

John Boy walked slowly up to Olivia, towering over her so she could take in the magnitude of his size. Her head only came to his chest. She still couldn't see any more of him now that he was closer than before. From the shadows under his cap he plucked a small toothpick from under his face mask and flicked it onto the ground at his boot-clad feet. He smelled of chewing tobacco and weeks of dried sweat.

"Now where's the fun in that, little chickadee?"

"You can't leave us defenseless. You can't leave us without our weapons," Axel all but pleaded with them, trying to talk some sense into these men.

"You know what?" John Boy said, turning to the rest of his crew as if he'd just had an epiphany. "The pup is right. Lem," he said, looking at the man who still gripped Olivia's bat. "Toss it, but don't make it too easy, OK?"

On command, the name he called Lem whipped the bat into the woods. Olivia heard it cut through the air with a whir, somehow avoiding the trees as it sailed further away from her.

"Grab the bag," John Boy said to one of the other men who quickly obliged.

Olivia's body shook violently but her brain worked hard to calm her down again. The worst was over. They had lost their stuff, their food and water. It might take her a while to recover her bat if it hadn't split on the trunk of a tree. But they could always find more food, more weapons, more stuff. The stores were abandoned, raided, but the world wasn't so scarce of resources yet that they couldn't recover from this night. Slowly, the further John Boy walked away with his back turned to her the more her body regained its control and stopped it's wracking.

Then John Boy spoke the words, "Kill the pup," and everything came crashing down.

During the prior chaos, when no one was paying attention, one of the men had retrieved Axel's sword from the ground and held it casually at his side. With full force, he thrust it straight through Axel's stomach and out the other side. Axel doubled and wrapped his hands around the protruding object with wide eyes that asked the question 'can this be real'? With a wild jerk, the man yanked back and retrieved his prize, wiping it off on his jeans. One by one they walked away, not even looking over their shoulders once to see if Axel was still alive or not.

Olivia let out a piercing cry. She felt as if her heart were being turned to ashes in her chest. She rushed over to Axel just as he fell to the ground, sprawled out on his back, clutching at his abdomen. His chest rose and fell in rapid, shallow breaths as the redness spread across his stomach to spill in little waterfalls onto the soft grass.

"Good luck, honey!" one of the men shouted as they turned their backs and stalked casually into the darkness of the woods. She heard their perverse chuckles fading with distance.

"Axel! Baby! Please, no. It's OK!" Olivia blurted out through the river of tears streaming from her eyes. "It's OK. We can get help. I can help you. You'll be fine. We just have to—" She reached out to yank him up by the arm but then simply touched his bicep gently with the tips of her fingers afraid anything stronger in force would cause him to perish right then and there. She sat helplessly at his side watching a single tear rival the slow and steady drip of blood from the corner of his mouth.

"They're—they're—" Axel struggled through the pain. "gone?"

"Yes," Olivia rushed to say before he finished so he wouldn't have to use any more of his energy to speak. "They're gone. They left." She took a few deep ragged breaths, letting it out in a heavy stream from between her lips. Her body was shaking violently again, so much so she feared she would drop dead herself. Her heart hammered against her ribcage with a ferocity that scared her.

"Liv," Axel said and then coughed, a splatter of blood left behind on his pale lips.

"I'm here," she said, placing her hand over his. She didn't even notice that almost immediately it was coated in hot, sticky blood. "What can I do?" she asked helplessly.

"Live," he said assuredly, firmly. "Just live. I love you." He tried to raise his hand from his wound to brush it against her face one last time. But his hand never made it. It fell to his side as his head lolled and his eyes closed, the only thing left moving the flow of red from his lips.

"No," Olivia whispered as her lip quivered. "No. Axel." She lowered her head onto his chest that no longer rose and fell, and she sobbed unrelentingly. She threw her arms around him, trying to embrace him one last time in case his last bit of essence was hanging on somehow. It was a nice thought. Her way of saying goodbye when she didn't know how. But there was nothing left of Axel but an empty shell, his life-force flowing from his wound and mouth until there was nothing left for him to give.

X

Olivia stayed the entire night by Axel's body, which was now cold, hard, and tinged the blueish-white of death. She clutched his hands and in the thin veil between awake and asleep she could have sworn a few times she felt his fingers twitch, but when the sun rose over the horizon and hit her face she knew it had not been true. Even in the warmth of the summer sun Axel's face was ashen white and his fingers were so stiff they couldn't be bent.

The entire night she had huddled in on herself with no shelter, no fire for light, no food though she couldn't have eaten anyway, and no water. It was the water that got her to her feet because she knew she wouldn't last long without it. But did she even want to last anymore? In what would be deemed the most horrible two days of her entire life she lost her mother and her boyfriend, her entire future in one fell swoop. Was there a way to come back from the horrors she'd seen and endured? For the briefest of seconds she considered ending it all right then and there, laying down next to Axel and dying beside him. But then she remembered they'd taken his sword and tossed her bat. She had nothing, no one. She was alone and soon she would be desperate and alone.

Though she pushed herself up onto her feet she remained crouched next to Axel, finding it impossible to let go of his hand knowing she had to leave him there on the bed of leaves in the woods. Her mind could not allow itself to wander and think of what would happen to him there. If she had the tools, the time, the strength, she would bury him but she had none of those things. She kissed the back of his hard cold hand and stood, turning away to face the sun and let it warm the coldness inside her that wanted to take over.

"Goodbye, Axel," she said beneath her breath, as if physical pain ensued from the very words she spoke.

She took a deep breath and let it burst out from her lips as one foot moved in front of the other. Even though it had been hectic and dark, she was sure of the direction the man had thrown her bat so she started there. Her eyes roamed the woods diligently, though the rest of her wanted to give up. How was she supposed to spot a natural wood bat amongst all the fallen tree branches and roots? Just then her foot kicked something buried beneath a rustle of leaves and dead grass that sounded different from the other bits of trees. She knelt down and uncovered her bat, her lucky bat that had once belonged to the mother she'd witnessed ripped to pieces, the mother who sacrificed herself so she and Axel could live just to have him die the very next day. Cradled in her hands as gently as if it were a newborn baby, Olivia let the tears flow down her cheeks in torrents. Her shoulders shook though a sound never escaped her pursed lips. Now that she had a weapon she had a chance. If she could locate some drinkable water she would be on the right path to survival. It was what her mother died for, what Axel died for, for her to live, so that was what she was going to do. She would take whatever it took to survive because she could not make their deaths meaningless.

For days she walked the same stretches of park, only venturing out when she was close enough to a store to see if there was any food, water, or supplies. In that time she found three cans of Spaghetti O's, some sugar free Gatorade, and a small pocket knife. One of the stores had a pharmacy but it had been so heavily picked over and all the names on the bottles were so unfamiliar to her that she left it all there, not wanting to do more damage than good by taking something when she didn't know what it was.

The dead multiplied every day. She didn't need access to the news to tell her that, if there was even such a thing as television or news anymore. In her head she kept track of the number of bodies she took down. The first day she was on her own she felled four. The next day seven. The day after that twelve. At this rate it was only a matter of time before she became overwhelmed. But surviving was surprisingly easier on her own than she thought it would be. When Axel was there he did most of the dirty work while she and her mother hung back and only swung when they had to. What she came to find in her first days of solitude was that bashing heads was cathartic. All those unanswered questions, all that pent up rage, it all came out against the undead and she lost that guilty feeling she used to have. These weren't people, they were monsters and monsters had to be destroyed. She wouldn't admit it to herself but she actually enjoyed it, that feeling of adrenaline as the bat connected with the brain was something she now craved.

When she wasn't defending herself she was testing out the vegetation around her. Food was sparser in the stores every day and with all the calories she burned with her constant movement her stomach craved more than a can of food a day. Grass was the worst and she refused to try that again, especially when she tasted the grit of dirt on the blades, or what she hoped was dirt. She was elated to find wild berries growing in a bush but then regretted it an hour later when she retched it all up. Apparently those berries were merely decorative and not meant to be consumed.

At night she spent her time up in the trees away from the munching mouths of the dead. When she climbed up, racing the setting sun to the highest, most comfortable branch before it sank beneath the horizon of Lake Michigan, she was reminded of her childhood in her quaint, quiet neighborhood where there were rows of perfect climbing trees and plenty of kids to climb them with on hot summer days. She rested her back against the thick trunk of the tree and let one leg hang down, swinging back and forth lazily. With her hands folded over her stomach she stared up at the canopy of leaves over her hoping for a quick glimpse of the evening stars above.

Sometimes the zombies would get wise and notice her up there and surround the tree. One night they stayed there until the sun rose again and she knew she would have to take care of the problem. They were relentless. She was more so, though, and she took out all five of them in under a minute. She was becoming deadly in her practice and she liked it.

But eventually the weight of endless wandering coupled with the lack of food and proper water caught up with her. That morning she felt a little lightheaded when she hopped out of the tree, landing on the ground on wobbly knees. The woods seemed to spin around her as she walked and a few times she ran right into a tree that seemed to dance around her. She opened her mouth to speak, not sure who she would be talking to, and then fell to the ground, everything around her going black.

When Olivia came to she was back in the bird sanctuary building behind the information desk. She was groggy and moaned with a terrible headache as she tried to sit up. It was dark but she knew the place well. In her confusion she expected to hear her mother coming out of the bathroom and to see Axel patrolling the front doors to make sure they were securely locked for the night. But she looked around and didn't see anyone. Was it all a dream? Had they been there the whole time and her mother and boyfriend were really alive and well? Her mind still reeled with exhaustion so it let her believe the lie for just a moment. And then an unfamiliar voice spoke.

"I think she's awake," it whispered in the blackness not too far away.

"Well don't just stand there, go make sure she's OK," a woman reprimanded.

The shuffling of feet grew louder as someone approached her. On instinct she smashed herself against the wall with nowhere to go. Her eyes squeezed shut tight and she felt around on the floor for her bat eagerly.

"It's OK, little darlin'," the man said. His voice was deep and gruff but also smooth and soothing.

Olivia opened her eyes and took in the face that was half-hidden in the darkness in front of her. He was a tall man with broad shoulders and a hulking girth. His hair was wavy, messy, and a beautiful rustic auburn. The same color ran through his beard which covered the entire lower half of his face with its bushiness.

"Are you hurt? Have you been bit?" he asked sincerely. She could tell he was more concerned with her well-being than anything else, like his own safety.

Olivia's eyes roved his figure, his face, his hands. When she concluded he wasn't a threat to her she relaxed the tension in her shoulders and shook her head. "No, I'm fine. At least I think I am. What happened?"

The woman who spoke before chimed in over the man's shoulder, resting her hands on him in a familiar way. "We found you passed out in the woods." Her voice was high and loud, louder than Olivia would have dared to speak in the midst of a zombie apocalypse in the middle of the night in a glass house. "Poor thing, you were just lying there like Sleeping Beauty or Snow White or somethin', untouched and peaceful looking."

Olivia certainly felt like Snow White in that moment, being woken up with a handful of strangers surrounding her like she was some alien figure, staring at her, prodding her with questions. She attempted to stand but her legs wobbled beneath her and she had to grip the wall for balance.

"Whoa there, little filly. Take 'er easy," the bearded man said as he mirrored her motion to stand, his arms outstretched to brace her if need be. "You should probably have some water and somethin' to eat before you try to move around."

"How long were you out there?" the woman asked, her green eyes turned down in concern.

"I—" Olivia started and then stopped. She had to take a moment to count in her head and think back to when it all started. This made her think of Maddie and Jennifer, her mother, Axel. It all came rushing back to her, ready to knock her off her feet. She slumped against the wall and let her legs turn to noodles like they begged to. She fell back to the ground in a heap. Those gathered around her all followed, dropping into squats around her with their hands outstretched in worry.

"I don't know. Since it started I guess," she said.

The woman looked to the man and exchanged silent words of shock with her wide eyes. "Honey, that was over a month ago. Are you saying you've been out there in the woods surviving on your own this entire time?"

Olivia opened her mouth to answer but then shut it again. Did she really want to go through her whole story, relive the tragically horrifying deaths of the people she loved most dearly in her life? It felt too personal for these unfamiliar faces. The forgiveness of her mother at the end, the deep burning love she had for Axel, the bond between her and Maddie and Jennifer that was almost like sisterhood; these were all pieces of her she was not ready to share with anyone. She wasn't sure she'd ever be ready, so she shook her head to let them know that yes, she had been out there alone.

"Oh, Rex," the woman said, one hand covering her mouth as tears gathered in her eyes, the other resting on the bearded man's shoulder.

"Well, you can stick with us as long as you like," the man called Rex said as he stood up. Everyone else in the group did the same and Olivia quickly realized that they hadn't been following her when she stood or collapsed, but the movements of their large, bearded leader.

"Thanks," she said meekly.

A young man in his thirties came over and handed Olivia a bottle of water and a paper plate piled with beans, hot dog chunks, and a little bit of mac n cheese mixed into it. Compared to what she'd been eating for the last week or so this looked like a gourmet meal. When he handed her a napkin underneath the plate she knew she must be dreaming.

"We'll let you be, give you some time to eat, adjust, and we'll talk more in the mornin'," Rex said with a smile hidden by the overhang of his mustache.

Olivia attempted to smile as she was already shoveling in the first bite of food she'd had in days, since...her mind quickly turned away from Axel and the pain thinking if him caused her now.

"Oh," the man said with a snap of his finger as if he had just remembered something important. "The only rules we got is no guns. The temptation to shoot is too great for some to bear. Best to keep it quiet and sneak through the darkness unheard." The imagery of the men sneaking up on her and Axel, waiting in the shadows of the night like malevolent ghosts out for nothing more than blood crossed her mind in a flash.

"I don't have a gun," was all she said, her voice muffled by the mouthful she was still chewing.

"Good girl."

As everyone scattered to return to their own corners of the building to hunker down for the night, Olivia quietly took stock of each of them. There was Rex, the defacto-leader who was larger than life and rugged. There was the woman Olivia assumed was his wife by their familiarity and ease with each other. She was almost comically small compared to Rex with platinum blonde hair pulled back into a high ponytail, her most likely grown out roots hidden beneath a camo baseball hat with a pink deer symbol stitched into it. She seemed trustworthy enough, at least so far. Her eyes, though a dull shade of green, were kind and caring. There was the younger man who handed her the food. He was well-built, not overly muscular but toned like Axel had been, though he was taller. His face was scruffy looking with the beginnings of a dark beard, his hair overgrown and disheveled as well. In one corner there was another man, dressed similarly as the others in jeans, a t-shirt, and a hat which he had pulled low over his face with his head rested back against the wall. His interest in Olivia and the commotion she caused seemed to be limited. Occasionally, whenever someone would make a louder than normal noise he would poke his hat up just enough to look out with one peering eye. When he saw all was in order he would pull it back down low and sit motionless as a marble statue. Back by the tanks of bugs and snakes was a man, likely in his forties, with a woman. They sat close enough for Olivia to realize they were together but not so close for her to recognize that they were husband and wife. They talked low but fast to each other. Every once in a while the woman would laugh and the man would shush her with laughter just beneath the surface. They were both natural blondes, both soft in their builds, and both dressed in dark jeans and dark shirts. Olivia reconsidered their togetherness and wondered if maybe they were brother and sister. It was hard to see their likeness with how dark it was.

Just then, a toilet flushed and she realized there was one more in the bathroom that she had yet to see. She had no idea if it was a man or a woman, but she hoped it was another female. That's when she realized that she was still nervous about the group. Another female paired with the lonely sleeping man was ideal because then that would mean every male there had a female counterpart they had to answer to. No one would give Olivia any trouble in that way…unless there were more out there scouting or wandering, returning to them at a later time. Olivia couldn't be sure of anything except she was sure she wasn't going to sleep a wink.

XI

Summer passed to fall and Olivia eventually found her place within the group of country folk that had found her. The wives were kind and took her under their wings in a sense, showing her what was good vegetation in the area and what was bad, how to sterilize water for drinking, how to sew, how to stab a zombie in the head with a knife. The person in the bathroom had turned out to be another man; one in his thirties and without a wife but neither of the single men gave her any trouble. In fact, they barely spoke to her or looked at her. They left her alone and that was the way she liked it.

The group worked together like a hive of bees. Everyone had their job. Olivia wished it had been according to skills and that she would be appointed lookout or scavenger, but unfortunately the group was a little more old-fashioned than progressive. Olivia was ordered to stay close with the wives, to learn what they taught her in cooking, repairing, mending, and berry picking. The men were the ones who went out to raid stores and homes, kill the surrounding zombie hordes that threatened the area, and kept watch over the building in shifts while everyone slept. In fact, it reminded Olivia of the caveman days, days of primitive cultures when a woman's job was to stay at home, rear children, gather and cook. The men were the hunters, heading out with their clubs in the hopes of dragging home a sabretooth tiger, or in this case a deer or a possum, which was a whole new dining experience for Olivia the first time that was dropped on her plate.

Any time she spent doing wifely duties with the others she longed for the life Axel had promised her; a life together in a home, protecting each other, loving each other.

"Did any of you have any kids?" she asked one day as the women walked the woods together, their arms hugging their midriffs for warmth as the wind shifted off the lake and threw a cool fall breeze at them.

"We did," Mary Beth, Rex's wife, said. "I had a girl about your age actually, or at least she would be." A heaviness settled in over them as each one remembered their lost children.

"What happened?" Olivia couldn't help asking. She knew the topic was sensitive and they might not want to talk about it, like she never ever spoke of Axel or her mother or friends, but she was curious and hoped thinking about it was more cathartic for them than it was for her.

"We lost her in the beginning. With all the craziness going on, everyone not having a clue what they were up against. Our house had been overrun and we were fighting to get out and…they just…they got her," she said softly, a catch in her voice which she cleared. "Rex never speaks of Cally, but I think it's good to talk. Helps us to not forget, to keep a piece of her alive within us." The other nodded in agreement but didn't seem eager to jump in with her own tragic stories.

"How about you," Mary Beth ventured, though she knew Olivia's answers were always guarded and vague. "Didn't you have a family at one point?"

Olivia couldn't help chuckling at the absurdity of the way the question was worded. "Of course I had a family," she laughed, throwing a stick she'd been fiddling with as far as she could. "My dad worked in the mills and my mom was a waitress. They weren't around when it all happened, though. I was home alone," she lied flawlessly, "so I have no idea what really happened to them."

"You never returned home to see if they ever came back?" Jillian, the blonde who looked so much like her husband they could be siblings asked.

"Well, I mean," Olivia stumbled for just a second but then collected herself again. "The house was destroyed by a horde that overtook it. There'd be nothing to come back to really. I'm pretty sure they're dead. There's no way they could have survived this." For a moment her mother's pleading face entered her mind, her voice urging her to run as the horde closed in on her. She swallowed the tears, something that had become easier with each passing day.

The only thing that ever unsettled Olivia was the amount of personal items the men would bring back from their raids. Some of the things could have been picked up at a store but not likely. One of the flannel shirts the men distributed to her had a name written on the tag; Katy. They could have picked it up at an abandoned house. But for some reason, something Olivia couldn't quite put her finger on, made her think something was wrong. It wasn't until a chilly night in October that she realized what it was exactly.

The men had just come back from a long excursion. In their backpacks and duffle bags, some new, they carried medical supplies, food, water, and winter clothes because there was no denying the bite in the air as temperatures dropped to the thirties at night. Snow was on its way and with that a whole new challenge to surviving the zombie apocalypse.

Olivia was with the women in the back of the glass building by the insects, rodents, and snake containment wall. Most of the creatures lay belly up since no one had remembered or cared to feed them or give them any water. The snake was the worst to see, curled in odd positions and stiff, its black and brown color faded to an ashen white. Its mouth hung open as if it died hoping one of them would drop a morsel of meat into its mouth.

"I would kill for a cookie right about now," Jillian complained with a grumble of her stomach. They were busy at work categorizing and storing what the men had brought home, making sure nothing was left out in the open. Anyone wandering the woods could peek inside and the point was to make the place look entirely empty and abandoned. The food was kept in the containment room where access to the cages was.

"Uhg, girl!" Mary Beth groaned with laughter hidden beneath it. "Don't even talk to me about sweets, OK? It feels like a year since I had any chocolate and I'm about to die."

It took every effort Olivia had not to roll her eyes at the innate conversation going on. They were in the middle of the end of the world, the extinction of humanity if they weren't careful, and these women were complaining about cookies and chocolate. How could they after what they've seen? Was it easier to pretend things weren't as bad as they were? She didn't know how anyone could. They were bad, and every day they were getting worse. The only silver lining to the colder weather was that it seemed to slow the dead down so it was easier to either get away or stop them in their tracks.

Just then Olivia heard a commotion at the front doors. All the women froze where they stood like deer in headlights, looking at the glass wall that led to the outside world. Rex and the other three men stood there, but there was someone else out there with them. Olivia couldn't quite make out who it was but she thought it was possibly a young woman with how quiet and meek she presented herself in the darkness. One of the men had a flashlight on him but he kept it pointed down at the ground as was their practice to not attract any unwanted attention. All Olivia could see was a pair of petite but dirty bare feet and long legs covered in hair and nothing else. They were muscular and had to be half-frozen in the night.

She couldn't hear what was being said exactly but she hoped that they would invite the poor woman in soon and give her something warm to eat like they had with her all those months ago. She feared the memories seeing another person who was out on their own would bring up for her but at the same time she was curious. It took a special type of person to be on their own in a world like this; a fighter, a warrior, an extremely smart individual. She wanted someone like that around her since she was quickly figuring out none of the women currently in the group had any of those attributes.

A scream followed by a deep groan filled the night air. Olivia threw down the box of rice she'd been holding, scooped up her bat that was leaning against the wall, and rushed toward the front door. She recognized the sound immediately; it was the sound of a young woman in pain. There was no hesitation in her mind as she made the decision to run to her rescue. A pair of arms wrapped around her, jerking her backwards and slamming her to the ground. In the confusion her fingers had loosened their grip on her bat and it went rolling noisily across the tile floor.

"Ah, ah, ah," the man married to Jillian said as he pinned her down by both her arms, strattling her without forgiveness. "This doesn't concern you, little girl."

Olivia struggled to get out of his grip but could barely move from the immense weight holding her down. She groaned and ground her teeth, hating the feeling of helplessness that overcame her. She squeezed her eyes shut and thrashed about uselessly. Meanwhile, the thuds and groans coming from a few short feet away, outside the open double glass doors, broke Olivia's heart to pieces. Why were they doing this? Why would they beat a poor woman looking for help? Who were these people?

The instant there was silence outside Olivia stopped moving, fearing the worst had been done and they had beaten the woman to death. For what? She didn't see the woman carrying anything. She looked like she barely had enough clothes on her to last another week in the cold let alone supplies to tempt this group.

"Stay down, pup!" A deep voice yelled.

Rex came strolling back in, a bounce in his step and big grin peeking out from beneath his beard. The other two men followed him back inside and secured the doors shut, leaving a shadowed heap on the trail behind them.

"Here you go, baby," Rex said to Mary Beth as she walked up to him, her eyes wide. Dangling from two fingers was a pair of red stilettos.

"Rex, are you serious?" Mary Beth asked. Olivia watched the interaction intensely from the ground. Mary Beth stared at the shoes with rounded eyes ready to bulge from her head. Olivia was sure she was about to explode, but she couldn't tell how. Something in her eyes told Olivia she wasn't mad as she should be, but delighted. Her lips upturned into a slow spreading grin. "Thank you, sweetie pie! I absolutely love them!"

Rex grinned, his hands shoved deep into his pockets. He rocked back and forth on his heels as if he were pleased with himself. "I knew you would, baby."

"I can't believe you remembered the one thing I missed most about the world were my red pumps," she said as her hand glided smoothly over the shiny surface of the stolen shoes. "You are so sweet."

Rex blushed. He actually blushed and looked down at his feet. "T'wasn't no big deal, babe. Anything for you."

She threw her arms around his neck and hugged him tightly, the red shoes dangling behind his back.

Olivia lay motionless on the floor now and the strong hold on her loosened. As the excitement settled and Mary Beth went off to show the other two women her prize, focus returned to her. Rex walked up to her, his steel-toed boots thudding on the hard tile floor. He knelt down, though he couldn't get eye level with her since she was still prone. He considered her long and hard.

"Now what's gonna happen now?" he asked and paused as if waiting for a reply, but Olivia had no idea what to say. Her head was still reeling from what she'd just seen. Who were these people she'd been living with? How could they do what they just did and how could she have no idea they were capable of it for months? When Olivia didn't respond he looked down at his hands and sighed. "OK, chickadee, here's how it's going to go. You're going to get up. Quietly. And you're going to go to your corner and sit there. Sleep, don't sleep. I don't really care. In the morning you're going to go about your day, you're going to gather food, you're going to chat with the ladies, you're going to try to grow some shit for us to eat, and then you're going to go to bed and do it all over again the next day. Are we on the same page here?"

She stared at him, hoping her eyes weren't too filled with hate. Tears gathered in the corners but she struggled against herself to keep them contained. She nodded her head in silence. Finally, the weight on her chest lifted. Before she could stop it she turned over and coughed as the sting of air returned to her lungs. She hadn't realized he'd been keeping her from taking full breaths as she lay there but it was all too apparent now as her body reacted to the new flow of oxygen.

Rex didn't reach down and cover her mouth or rush to shut her up. He simply turned his head and gave a look to no one in particular that said he thought Olivia was pathetic just then, hacking and gulping for air. He stood and gazed over her, as if he expected her to follow his lead. She did, and she did her best to stand upright though there was a sharp pain in her back from where she'd been smashed against the floor. She reached behind and touched the tender spot on the lower left side of her back and winced. That was going to be a nasty bruise in the morning if it wasn't already.

Without anything more to say on either side, Olivia walked slowly and awkwardly with pain to the corner behind the information desk like a wounded puppy. As that analogy ran through her mind she suddenly stopped in her tracks and straightened right up. Her whole body stiffened. Puppy. Pup. That's what the men who murdered Axel called him before they killed him. That's what someone had just called this woman after they jumped her for her shoes. Sweat broke out on her forehead and under her arms as her stomach churned with realization. She wasn't sure if she wanted to hurl or collapse so she just stood there in shock. The only ounce of bravery she had left in her compelled her to look over her shoulder at Rex standing by the front door. She tried to picture him in overalls, a baseball hat, cloaked in more darkness than he was now.

She whirled back around to stare at the wall with wide eyes. Her hand slapped over her mouth without her telling it to as the tears flowed freely without permission. It was them. They were the ones. She'd been living with them for months and never saw it, never recognized his voice, never recognized his form or face or anything. And as far as she knew they hadn't recognized her. It was pitch black that night, the only light shining upward in a beam into the trees from the flashlight that had gotten kicked over in the scuffle to point at nothing at all. It was near impossible to distinguish any one person from another except by the light of the moon that sometimes shone through the leaves to reveal living shadows fighting with each other. It was chaos. Her mind remembered it in bursts of action and panic and nothing more. How could she have recognized them?

Olivia lowered her hand, walked behind the information desk, and sat on the floor with her back pressed against the wall. She didn't make a sound but hoped that she blended in with the background and that soon the others would forget about her display of passion against their violent crime. She hoped they settled in soon and laid their heads to rest, because it would be the last time they ever did so.

XII

Olivia lay in waiting for hours. She curled up on the floor and covered herself with a jacket Mary Beth had given her from one of Rex's runs. She couldn't help being disgusted as the wool touched her body, knowing someone probably suffered or died in order for her to be warm that night. One by one the group found their spots and settled in. Rex hadn't forgotten her display earlier and walked by the desk every once in a while to check on her, make sure she wasn't sitting there, stewing, and plotting her revenge like she was. To anyone who saw, she was fast asleep. Eventually, he too sat next to his wife, put her head in his lap, and leaned his own back against the wall.

Silence overtook the glass center so the only sound was the outside woods surrounding them; crickets that clung to the world despite the biting cold that was moving in, the yips of coyotes far off in the distance on the hunt. It all went unheard by Olivia, whose eyes popped open with one intent; to get her revenge. There were a few things she knew that would be to her advantage; the first being the group did not believe in guns. Too noisy, which was good advice in a moment like this. She was clearly outnumbered so she couldn't wake the others while she was taking care of the first one. She also knew that the couples slept close together so she could quickly do them both at the same time. As she systematically thought these things out her emotions started to creep in to best her.

How could she so cold-heartedly think about murdering an entire group of people? The very thing she hated them for she was contemplating doing herself. And as if in answer she saw Axel before her as he'd been when he was alive; his slender lethal body, his nose and cheeks speckled with light freckles, his crooked playful grin that made her stomach flutter with excitement, the way his skin felt warm against hers when he held her close. And then, without warning, she saw Axel standing there, mouth agape, sword protruding from his belly. Her jaw clenched tight to the point she thought her teeth would shatter, but she couldn't help it. A fire burned within her and grew in intensity as the vision of Axel's death refused to disperse. Her body started shaking, clenching and convulsing with fury.

Slowly, she pushed herself up onto her elbow and looked around the room. There was no movement, no light, nothing to signify anyone was still awake. She pushed herself up further until she was crouched on her feet, peering around the edge of the desk, her hand groping the darkness for her bat that always lay by her side. Her heart raced as she felt nothing on the floor or against the wall. In moments, her eyes adjusted from being closed and she realized it was no longer there. She must have actually fallen asleep and that's when Rex came over and took her bat. A curse flew to her lips but she bit it back as she stood fully. There was only one place it could be and that was locked away behind the reptile cages with the food.

To keep order the food and weapons had always been placed under lock. It was a simple padlock someone might use for their storage unit. It fit so perfectly she wondered if it wasn't the one that originally came on the door and they happened to find the key in a drawer somewhere. It would have been easy for her and Axel and her mother to overlook that since it wasn't something they were looking for at all when they came to this place. She had two options; find the key and unlock it, or break into it. Both did not sound easy or optimal. Breaking into it could be loud, she could wake someone up in the process of fumbling, it could take a long time to do. But taking the key would be a challenge especially since it most likely was on Rex or Mary Beth's person. No, that definitely was not an option.

Quietly, precisely, she opened the drawers of the desk and searched through them until she found something that might work; a hairpin. She straightened it out and then tiptoed over to the door that led behind the cages. Normally, the brother-sister or husband-wife duo slept over there but tonight they decided to bask in the glow of the moonlight by the window to the bird sanctuary across from the cages. It was set up perfectly. It was meant to be. She had to destroy these people before they killed again. There were man-eating zombies out there after all doing a number on humankind. There was no need for people pulling the same crap.

She snuck over to the pantry-slash-weapon's closet and worked at the lock with the hairpin. This was a moment where she actually missed modern technology. A YouTube video on how to pick a lock sure would come in handy. But she wouldn't give up as she twisted and wiggled the pin until she heard a distinct click that sent her heart racing. Her face tightened into a strained grin as she tried to remain soundless in the dead of night. Slowly, carefully, she peeled back the door and went inside, closing it until just a crack was left. If anyone woke up and looked that way they wouldn't know the difference but she could still make a quick exit without making more sound than she already had.

Inside the pantry it was pitch black. She pulled out the little pocket flashlight she'd always kept on her and pointed it ahead. Blinding light reflected off something on the back wall and shone across her face. She shielded her eyes on instinct. Once she was able to collect herself and clear the floating spots from her vision she lowered the light just a bit and saw what it was that had tried to blind her; Axel's sword. She would have recognized it anywhere. She'd seen it countless times as they tried to survive in the woods together, day in and day out for a month. It was slightly curved, the silver of the blade gleaming almost white. The hilt was black and had gold inlay of something in Korean she did not know. She never got the chance to ask him if he knew. As she stared at the sword she wished she'd had more time for things like that with him. Her chest tightened. She sniffed quietly and composed herself. Now wasn't the time for that.

She grabbed the sword, a bowie knife, her bat which was propped against the wall next to Axel's sword, fittingly. With so much running through her mind she turned to leave but then thought better of it. If everything went according to plan there wouldn't be anyone to eat the food in this pantry, she thought. And then she grabbed a backpack shoved in the corner on the floor and shoved canned food, water bottles, pre-packaged snacks, and whatever else she could get her hands on and reasonably carry away into the night.

And that was it. She was done preparing. It was now time to act.

Olivia made quick and quiet work of the group. She started with the man who always slept alone, closing his mouth with her hand as she dragged the jagged knife across his tender throat. As he struggled, his eyes wide and his moans dying somewhere deep within his chest, she laid him down with one hand as the other, drenched in blood, stayed firmly on his lips. She then moved to the only other single man, finishing him off in the same way since it proved to be quick and silent. After each slice she stuck her head up like a prairie dog to make sure no one had heard anything. No movement. No sound. Nothing. She was safe.

Next, she moved onto the couples, starting with Jillian and her husband. They both lay on the floor, their head cushioned on makeshift pillows made of sweatshirts. They lay head to head with their fingers intertwined by their faces on the floor. To anyone else it would have looked sweet, almost romantic, like an oil painting from Ancient Rome. But all she saw was the man who helped to bring about Axel's death, who left her stranded with no one and no way to protect herself against the dead, and a wife that approved of all her husband did cold-heartedly. With the bottom of her bat, using the little ball at the end used to help place the hands for proper gripping, she raised it up high and brought it down on both their temples, one after another, with a sickening crunch. There were no moans, no struggles, no moments of panic from either of them. With a sound smaller than she would have imagined, they were simply gone. She stared down at them and the blood seeping from the dent in their heads and felt nothing. It was such a relief, a moment of rest from the continuous agony she felt from the horrifying way she lost Axel.

She saved Rex and Mary Beth for last because in her eyes they were the worst. They led the group in these terrible acts, they encouraged murder for plunder, they squealed for joy when they saw someone abused to the point of death all for a pair of useless shoes. They had to go. But as she approached the sleeping giant she realized something that sent her stomach plummeting down to her feet. Mary Beth wasn't there.

In a moment of panic, Olivia whirled around as if she'd find the woman standing behind her ready to kill her for what she'd done, but no one was there. Where was she? Olivia was certain now that she had definitely fallen asleep by accident as she lay in wait. Stupid! She chastised herself as she wracked her brain for what to do next. "OK," the voice in her head said hurriedly, "It's best to just take care of Rex now and then I only have to deal with Mary Beth when she makes herself known. She's probably outside for some reason or in the bathroom. Who knows? But I have to find her and finish this. She can't be the only one left. Unless that would be poetic justice for her. Really it should be Rex who's left alone with all his loved ones murdered before him. That's how he left me that terrible night." It was decided. There was no turning back. If she left now Rex and Mary Beth wouldn't stop until they found her.

She raised her bat as if she were stepping up to the plate. There was no use in being quiet now. Everyone else in the room except her and Rex were dead, and soon he would join them. Her grip was tight, her elbows raised high, her breathing long and slow though her heart was racing. With a crack, she knocked him sideways. The big man groaned and slowly with a jerk raised his hand to his head, as if he were a malfunctioning robot. She knew even if she left now there would be no coming back from the blow he'd just been dealt. But she couldn't stop herself. She struck again and again and again until he was unrecognizable, just a heaping mess on the floor. Standing over him, she heaved great gulps of breaths from the exertion and the adrenaline.

Just then she heard a toilet flush. It brought her back to herself and she crouched down, walking low and close to the wall so she might not be seen if Mary Beth came out. She crept around to the public restroom. In the same way she opened the pantry door she slowly and cautiously entered the bathroom. All the stall doors were closed but it was clear which one Mary

Beth was in. The toes of two red pumps stuck out from underneath the middle one, tapping as if she were listening to a jaunty tune, completely unaware of what had just happened outside her bathroom stall.

Olivia prepared the end of her bat and slammed it into the stall door, busting it wide open with a great crash. Mary Beth's eyes shot wide open as she braced herself against the walls with her hands. Her pants were down around her ankles and there was a terrible smell emanating from her. Olivia raised her bat above her head since it was the only way to strike. She hesitated for just a second, not sure if she could go through with it, with Mary Beth's eyes looking up into hers with fear. But then she saw Axel and she knew there was no question anymore. It had to be done. They couldn't be allowed to keep doing this. Mary Beth turned her head away and when Olivia brought it down it smashed against her temple and killed her instantly. Her body slumped to the side she was leaning into until her face was smashed against the stall wall.

It was done.

She could leave now knowing the death of her love, of Axel, was avenged. That those people got what they deserved for being cold-blooded murderers. Only the tiniest whisper inside of her wondered if this made her a cold-blooded murderer too. But as she walked out she collapsed on the hard tile, her bat hitting with several clanks as it rolled away. The gravity of what she'd done slammed against her like a tsunami, threatening to drown her in guilt and regret.

"I'm no better," she said to no one, though her echo seemed to answer her in faint agreement. She retched on the floor, unable to keep down the bile in her stomach from rising until she had emptied it completely. She let her body slump against the wall like it wanted to, begged to, couldn't help but doing. Her chest rose and fell in heavy heaves as her mind raced with an endless string of berating words that rang so loudly in her mind that she thought she could actually hear them. She threw her hands over her ears and curled into a ball on the floor, rocking back and forth as if that would soothe her. She knew it wouldn't. Nothing would. She thought getting revenge would make her feel better but it only made her feel worse, and worst of all it didn't bring Axel back...nothing would.

Exhaustion took over her and she didn't open her eyes again until the glint of sunlight danced across her eyelids in the morning. Slowly, she pushed herself up and stood. She stared into the open room with her lips parted, her energy drained and her will to continue on waning. It hadn't been a rage-filled nightmare. Scattered on the floor were the bodies of the men and women she'd brutally killed. She was sure this was the moment she would have a breakdown, crumbling into uncontrollable tears, waiting there in the fetal position until the zombies found her and devoured her, but that's not what she felt at all.

She felt nothing.

She was numb.

And all she knew was that no matter where she ventured, where she laid roots or wandered, she was never going to trust a group of strangers ever again. The only way she would make herself part of a group again was if she knew someone in it from the world before. That was the only way to make sure she didn't fall prey to the new and unforgiving world that was now her reality.

Read Dead Soil next and start the series that's made it onto multiple Amazon Bestseller lists!

Prologue

I looked down at the journal in my hands and gave it a squeeze. A smile spread across my weary face. We might not have the key to ending this plague. There's no guarantee we will all make it to Chicago alive. Some of us could die trying to get there. We could all die. But we're going to try. We have to.

Part One

"The nation that destroys its soil destroys itself."

—Franklin D. Roosevelt

I

The shooting range Liam Scott took his fiancée to was nothing more than targets set up on a local farmer's home acreage. Tight knit piles of hay sat ten feet high in neat rows. Attached to the middle and swaying slightly in the light summer breeze were crudely cut pieces of wood with red and white bullseyes painted on them.

There was no one else there to watch as Christine Moore attempted to practice archery for the first time. It was peaceful to be somewhere so remote after five days in the bustle of the Chicago Loop, where the firm she worked at for the last four years was located. Every day she found a reason to be thankful she'd decided to stay in northwest Indiana instead, even if she had to commute an hour and fifteen minutes each way to work.

Christine closed her eyes and drew in a deep breath of thick, hot air while Liam set up their spot in front of an end target. The scents of freshly cut grass, stale hay, and the water of Lake Michigan wafted up her nostrils. They reminded Christine of her childhood and where she grew up along the scenic route of highway twelve, which wasn't far from where she stood.

"Arrows used to be made out wood, of course, but now they make them out of aluminum," Liam Scott said in his cool British accent as he dove right into his role of teacher for the day. "Now the bow is made up of this piece here."

He pointed to the curved solid limb. "And the bow string, here."

Christine cocked her head to the side, her big blue eyes glazed over. One minute in and she was bored with the lesson. "I didn't come here to learn the anatomy of a bow. We could've done that at home. I came to shoot."

"How are you supposed to *release* the arrow if you don't even know how the bow works?" Liam's voice was loving with just a hint of condensation.

"It's not rocket science, sweetie," Christine shot back in the same tone. "You pull back and you let go."

"That's Doctor Sweetie to you." Liam gave a coy smile.

Christine let out a huff of laughter. "Doctor of plants. And that doesn't mean you know everything either. I know what I'm doing."

"By all means." Liam Scott grinned and held the bow out to his fiancée.

Christine snatched it from his hands with a confident smile, her chin raised slightly toward the unyielding sun. With her feet planted firmly on the ground, perpendicular to the target, she readied the arrow. She drew back and heard a soft snort from behind her. Ignoring Liam as best she could, she concentrated on her hold. It required more effort than she thought it would. It took all her strength to keep her arms from shaking under the pressure.

Even with the trembling, there was still no doubt in her mind that she would be able to hit the target. She envisioned the arrow piercing the solid red middle of the bullseye. She didn't want Liam to know how much she struggled to hold the arrow steady.

Christine Moore loved Liam Scott unconditionally, but sometimes he treated her like a fragile doll. If he didn't think she could learn to shoot, then why did he bring her there in the first place? She wanted to show him she was just as capable as he was, that he didn't have to protect her all the time. They could protect each other. She shook her head and her long, blond ponytail swung at her back. It wasn't medieval times. What would they ever use a bow and arrow for aside from practice shooting? What were they practicing for?

Liam Scott stood a ways behind his fiancée with his thin arms folded over his chest. The summer breeze blew his ginger hair freely as the sun beat down on his neck. He could feel his fair skin prickle with the beginnings of a burn.

He watched Christine stare at the target with more dedication and concentration than he'd seen her give anything else in the five years he'd known her, and that included the time he sneaked into court and watched her take down the CEO of a fortune five hundred company for embezzlement. A crooked smile spread across his face. It didn't matter if she hit the target or not. They were sharing an honored Scott tradition together and she was actually taking it seriously, even if it was only to prove him wrong.

The longer Christine tried to hold the arrow steady, Liam's mind wandered to his father. He was the one who had started the birthday target practices back when they lived in Liverpool. Even his mother joined them on her birthday. They did it every year until his parents' fatal car accident when Liam was only nine. None of his foster parents had bothered to take him on any of his following birthdays. It warmed his heart to carry the tradition on with the woman who was going to be his wife and the mother of his children.

Christine Moore made one last attempt to pull the arrow further back to ensure it would make it all the way to its target. With a soft exhale, her fingers released the arrow. It seemed to move in slow motion as it cut through the heavy air to land in the mess of hay beneath the target board.

She immediately turned to Liam. Her face was flushed with embarrassment. She silently waited for him to rub her defeat in her face.

"When I first tried I came this close to shooting the man at the target next to us in the foot," he said as he held his thumb and index finger as closely together as possible without touching.

Christine walked over to him and wrapped her arms around his neck with the bow still clutched in her hand.

He laughed into her soft, wavy hair. "Mind you, I *was* only five at the time."

She pulled away and slapped him on the chest. They both gave in to laughter.

"Want me to show you the proper way now?" he asked, but not in a condescending way that said he knew better than her.

It was genuine and Christine knew she could say no if she wanted to without any hard feelings between them. That was just how Liam was and, after all, it was *her* birthday.

She smiled up at him, her neck bent all the way back to stare into his light-green eyes. "Thank you for making me a part of your family today."

Liam Scott smiled back down at her. He took the bow from her hand, picked up an arrow, and drew it back with ease. With the quick release of his fingers, he let it go. The arrow shot straight into the bullseye.

II

Allison Murphy gallivanted around Christine and Liam's apartment for hours as she hung streamers and balloons from wherever she could reach. Confetti littered the floor in metallic clumps. She wasn't worried about the cleanup the next day, only about making the surprise party amazing for her dearest friend and colleague.

She jumped when someone knocked at the door. The guests had started to arrive and she still hadn't found the wine and Champaign glasses to set up on the buffet table. Quickly, she raced to the kitchen and wrenched open all the cabinets. She should have brought her own glasses. Tupperware and white paper napkins scattered the floor as she swiped them out of the way. In the far back next to the slow cooker there was a box of assorted plastic party glasses. It would have to do.

There was another series of knocks, more impatient and aggressive. "Just a minute!" she yelled. She turned on her heels as she squat on the floor with clear Tupperware gathered in her arms. She shoved them back in the cabinet and shut the door before they could come tumbling back out.

Within a half hour the small one bedroom apartment was packed.

"Shh!" Allison Murphy hushed the twenty or so people as she peeked through the blinds at the parking lot below. "They're coming! Hide!"

"Hide where?" Sylvia Goldstein asked in her thick New York accent. "This place is like a sardine can."

Allison rolled her eyes and knelt beside the couch, still in clear view of the doorway. Her ankles wobbled on her thin high heels. Hushed giggles filled the darkness as Christine Moore's voice echoed through the open hallway outside.

"We're home!" Liam yelled.

Christine looked at him like he was off his rocker. There was tenderness hidden behind her scrunched eyes. She knew what was waiting for her on the other side of the door. They walked into the apartment holding hands. Christine flipped the light switch on in the entryway.

"Surprise!" everyone shouted as they jumped up from their hiding spots.

Christine screamed and smacked her hands over her mouth as her blue eyes bulged. The apartment looked like a wishy-washy teenage girl's sweet sixteen party with pink streamers, balloons, vinyl tablecloths, and paper plates covering every surface. Multicolored confetti littered the floor and permeated the carpet. It wasn't Christine's taste in the least. She'd never been the girly-girl type. But she genuinely smiled when she saw it, because she knew it was absolutely Allison Murphy.

"Happy birthday, love," Liam said and kissed her forehead.

Christine looked at all her friends with a gaping smile. There were a few people mixed in she'd seen around before, but didn't know personally, a couple she didn't know at all, and then there were her parents. Even though they were involved in her life, she was still surprised to see them there. Parties weren't really their thing. Parties weren't really Christine's thing either, but Liam seemed so excited to throw one for her that she kept her mouth shut about it.

Lidia Moore walked over to her daughter and cupped her face in her hands and kissed her on the cheek. "I can't believe you're twenty-eight already," she said with misty eyes. "It's like I blinked and you were grown."

Christine's mouth pulled into a smile only a daughter could give her mother when she thought she was being overly sentimental. "Mom…"

"I'm sorry. You're right," Lidia Moore said as she sniffed back her tears and dabbed at her eyes. "It's a party. Your father's here too," she added as if he hadn't been standing right beside her the entire time.

Thomas Moore leaned in and gave Christine a tight, one-armed hug as she wrapped both her arms around his waist. He smelled faintly of cigar smoke and potting soil. He'd no doubt spent the day working in their backyard garden, a hobby he'd taken to after retirement from the iron-workers union.

"I'm really glad you both came," Christine said.

Lidia Moore leaned in close to her daughter's ear as her eyes lingered on Liam. "He's a good man," she whispered. "Take care of him."

Christine nodded her head and smiled at her fiancé, who was talking to some of the other guests. "I will," she said to her mother. "I'm going to go say hi to everyone—"

Her mother nodded zealously before she finished speaking. "Go, go, mingle. It's your party. We'll be here."

Christine walked over to Liam and looped her arm through his. They were still in their jeans and t-shirts from the range. She felt his warm, burnt skin on her bare arm and felt relaxed.

"Happy birthda-a-a-ay, girl!" Carolyn Bock, the younger woman from upstairs, said with a crooked smile and an almost empty Champaign glass in her hand.

Christine had only met Carolyn once before when Liam suggested they get together because they were both relatively close in age, ignoring the fact that they had absolutely nothing in common except the color of their hair. Carolyn Bock was a twenty-six year old office girl at the local steel mill. She was surrounded by good old country boys and loved every minute of it. Christine was a corporate lawyer at a firm in downtown Chicago. She wore a nice suit, carried a briefcase, and didn't say things like "ya'll" or "bitchin'".

"Thanks. Glad you could make it," Christine said as her eyes drifted to the mousy-looking woman standing next to Carolyn.

"This is Debbie Henson. She lives next door to me. I hope it's OK I brought her along. I thought she could use a wild night out," Carolyn said as she nudged the meek woman with scraggly red hair.

Debbie looked around nervously. She let out a hoarse laugh and then cleared her throat. "Nice to meet you. Happy birthday," she said just above a whisper. Her eyes shifted around the apartment as if she expected the boogeyman to pop out and snatch her away.

Christine only knew Debbie by her last name. She'd heard stories about the fights she and her husband had late at night. She noticed the small, scabbed-over split in Debbie's lip and wondered if that was his doing.

"Thank you, both," Christine said politely. "Enjoy!"

Carolyn raised her glass and threw back what little alcohol was left in it, draining it down to the very bottom.

"The look on your face!" Allison Murphy yelled as she wrapped Christine in a tight hug. "It was priceless. We got her!" She shoved Liam playfully on the shoulder.

He gave a quick laugh. "Yes, we did. She didn't have the slightest clue."

Christine smiled and looked away as she sipped from her glass. She'd seen an email from Liam on Allison's computer a week ago that discussed the plans for her surprise party. She was glad her practiced shock had fooled them both. She'd hate to disappoint her fiancé.

Liam spotted Zack Kran, his friend and neighbor, from across the room and gestured his head several times toward Allison.

The girls looked at each other through squinted eyes and Christine shrugged her shoulders.

Zack, a thin man with a groomed beard and a tight button-down shirt, caught sight of Liam and gave him two thumbs up before meandering over. "Oh, hey!" he said. "Happy birthday, Chris. Almost thirty!"

"Don't remind me," she huffed.

"Hey, I take offense to that. Thirty's not so bad," Zack said with a hearty chuckle.

Liam jumped in before either of the women could roll their eyes. "Zack this is Allison. Allison…*this* is Zack."

The two shook hands awkwardly as Allison looked to her friend with pleading eyes.

Christine pinched the arm of Liam's shirt and pulled him aside. "What are you doing?" she asked as she tried not to laugh. "You know Allison's married, right?"

"No! Isn't that something you should tell your fiancé about your best friend?"

Christine looked at him hard. "She is *not* my best friend. She's just…my only ally at work."

Allison looked over her shoulder at Christine while Zack laughed at his own joke, her brown eyes wide with animosity. Christine couldn't help giving Allison a thumbs up in mockery. Allison slipped her middle finger up discreetly when Zack wasn't looking. Christine laughed. Then, her face fell. Allison was undeniably her best friend.

"Oh, shit. When did that happen?"

"It's only natural," Liam answered in his best therapist voice, which he always used when proving a point. "She was your mother hen when you first arrived at the firm and since then you two have grown accustomed to relying on each other for comfort and familiarity in a place you both despise."

"Yeah? Well your best friend rides a skateboard to the comic book store every day and has a beard like Grizzly Adams," Christine retorted.

"Zack *owns* the store. It's not like he simply hangs out there daily."

They both broke into laughter simultaneously. Having Allison as a best friend wasn't the worst thing in the world Christine decided. Her short, brown bob always laid perfectly above her shoulders, never a hair out of place. She wore the most expensive high heels Christine had ever seen and never stumbled as she walked flawlessly in them. Her beautiful suits hugged her tight and made it look like she had curves on her thin, straight body. Not only was she Christine's friend…Christine looked up to her. The last person she'd ever looked up to was her sister and she hadn't seen her since she took off when she was eighteen and Christine was still in the tenth grade.

Christine's mood sobered in the flicker of a heartbeat. "Hey, did you happen to invite my sister?"

Liam's face fell. "I passed the invitation along for her to your parents, but they said she never responded. Last they heard from her, she was in California selling hats on the boardwalk or something. I'm not sure," he said softly.

Christine stared for a moment at the carpet and blinked to clear her eyes. She looked at the small black butterfly tattooed on the underside of her right forearm. The ink of the crooked wings was faded from years of neglect. She touched a finger to it and then looked away. "It's fine," she assured Liam with a contrived smile. "It's fine. I should know better by now."

"She left a long time ago," he said as he put a hand on her shoulder. Liam saw her eyes flicker to her arm again. "How about a drink?" He reached over to the buffet table and grabbed a bottle of wine and a glass. He filled it to the brim.

"Thanks," she said, "I just need to go to the bathroom."

He nodded his head slowly.

Christine shut the door behind her and set her glass on the bathroom counter. As she stared in the mirror, she thought about how different she and her sister had looked from each other as children and what she must look like now. Was she taller, thinner, heavier, tanner? Had her butterfly tattoo faded as much as Christine's had? She shook her head and blinked a few times. None of it mattered. She was probably never going to see her sister again.

She emerged from the cramped bathroom and almost ran right into Sylvia Goldstein, the last person she wanted to see. Why had Liam invited her and her husband after their disastrous double date?

"Great party!" Sylvia said in her loud, nasally voice. "It's quite a group you've put together. So many people here in this tiny apartment!"

"Thanks. It was all Liam's—"

"And you still don't look a day over twenty-one. *What* is your secret?" Sylvia interrupted as she raised a hand to her dark, bouffant hair to make sure it was still in place.

"Actually," Christine said as she nudged her way past Sylvia. "Would you excuse me? I have to say hi to…" she looked around the room for someone available. She spotted an old woman with white hair sitting alone on the bay window seat. Christine pointed to her and walked away without another word. Once Sylvia's back was turned, Christine changed her course for Liam.

"Hey," she leaned in to whisper. "Who brought the Golden Girl?"

Liam stared blankly back.

"*The Golden Girls*? Blanch? Rose? Nothing? Let me try again. Who brought the old woman sitting by the window?"

He turned to look and his green eyes lit up with recognition. "Oh, that's Ralph Sherman's mother-in-law. Her flat's on the ground floor."

She smiled. Flat. His British accent got her every time. "And who's Ralph Sherman?"

Liam gazed around the room until he spotted Ralph and his wife, Sally, who held their nine-month-old daughter in her arms while she talked to Ben and Sylvia Goldstein. Liam pointed them out with a slight nod of his head. Sylvia gave an enthusiastic wave before Christine could look away and pretend she hadn't seen her.

"And how do we know him?" she asked.

"He's the kid who installed our cable and internet when we moved in." Liam raised his glass to Ralph when their eyes met.

"Oh." She didn't remember him. How could these people live in the same building as her for a year and she still had no idea who they were? And why did Liam know everyone?

As if Christine's thoughts were written across her face, Liam looked at her with soft eyes. "You've been really stressed with work, staying late at the office…It's hard to get to know people with those hours."

She nodded, but was still lost in thought. Maybe it *was* her fault she didn't have any real friends. She'd always preferred time alone as opposed to being surrounded by people. That was just who she was, until she met Liam during her last semester at school. Then, all she wanted to do was spend time with him when she wasn't working. She didn't have time for much else.

Liam could tell his fiancée was stuck inside her own head by the glossy, vacant look on her face. He was determined to get her out to enjoy the party, maybe even make some new friends. "Yeah, I feel bad for the whole lot of them actually," he said as he looked back at Ralph. "They don't get out much because his wife is always at home with the baby or taking care of her mother. Seems like she could really use a companion. Someone to expand her horizons a bit, or just to talk to…" He trailed off when he saw the stern look on Christine's face.

"You promised me no more blind friend-dates," she hissed. "Not after *Sylvia Goldstein*." She spat the name out like it was a rancid piece of meat. "You've lost all hook-up privileges."

Liam laughed and threw his arm over her shoulder to reel her in. "How about another drink?" He turned to walk to the buffet table, but his path was blocked.

"Looks like we're going to have to get going," Dr. Ronald Conrad, Liam's colleague, said with his wife at his side. Her cheeks were burning bright red and she kept tugging at the sleeve of her husband's crisp blue shirt.

"Everything all right?" Liam asked.

"Yeah, it's just Gloria, here, installed one of those nanny-cams, y'know, to see what Olivia was up to when we're not home. Turns out the minute we left she put the baby to bed and invited her delinquent boyfriend over."

Liam stretched his mouth back and grit his teeth in a show of pained sympathy. "Sorry, mate."

"No matter. It's this one who's all bent out of shape now because she caught this kid plowing her seventeen-year-old niece."

"They weren't having sex!" Gloria Conrad screeched. She turned to Liam and spoke to him directly. "They had their clothes on."

He nodded his head and opened his mouth, but was at a loss for what to say.

"Great party," Gloria said as she touched Liam lightly on the arm and then turned in a flurry to head for the door. Ronald scurried after her.

"She's…" Christine said as the Conrads hurried off, "…passionate."

"Right," Liam laughed. "Well said."

"When is Ronnie being transferred out to Stanford?"

Liam shrugged his shoulders. "He hopes soon. He hates it here."

"Why's that?"

"He thinks Dr. Hyde uses him like an errand boy. I mean, the man's got a doctorate in microbiology. He shouldn't be picking up the dry cleaning."

"And Dr. Hyde is your new boss?"

"Correct," Liam said with a nod. "He invited me to join his team to create a vaccine for that new strain of flu everyone's on about."

Christine nodded her head. She tried to remember when Liam had told her all this, but she couldn't. She did, however, remember all the breaking news over the deadly flu. It was hard to miss. If they weren't interrupting shows to update everyone, it scrolled slowly across the bottom of the screen on every local channel.

"They project it to wipe out almost forty percent of the population if someone doesn't make a working vaccine soon."

"What's taking so long?" Christine asked with a furrowed brow.

Liam gave a discordant laugh. "It's not that simple. Every time we think we've got it, the flu strand changes and we have to start all over. That's why almost every lab in the country is working around the clock to stop it. They just…can't."

Christine let Liam's word drift in and out of her mind as the wine hit her all at once. Unexpectedly, a ball of panic dropped in her stomach and weighed it down like a bowling ball. Forty percent of the population could be wiped out in one year because of something as common as the flu. Maybe she should consider getting one of those disposable hospital masks, even though it creeped her out when she saw someone walking around in one.

Over the next twenty minutes, people said their goodbyes. The crowd dissipated until it was only Liam, Christine, Luke Benson from upstairs, and Carolyn Bock left.

Luke claimed he wanted to help the couple clean up, but it was his anxiety over Carolyn cornering him at his apartment door that kept him there. She had jumped at the chance to offer to help clean once he had. Her eyes lingered on him whenever he bent over to pick up a dropped plate or napkin. She watched his dark skin tighten over his rounded arm muscles and sighed.

Each time, he looked to Liam and Christine with wide, desperate eyes.

"Poor guy," Christine cooed in a whisper to Liam. "We should help him."

Liam nodded and opened his mouth to speak, but was cut off by the muffled sounds of shouting from the floor above. Everyone looked up in silence.

"I better go," Carolyn said immediately and dropped the trash that was in her hand before she darted out the door. She left it open behind her.

The warm breeze from the open hallway wafted up Christine's nose, bringing the scent of the Dunes and Lake Michigan along with it. A vision of her grandmother picking wildflowers along the Calumet bike path swam through her fermented mind. She missed her so much, even though she died almost ten years ago. The woman had practically raised her while her parents immersed themselves in their work.

A faint knock, only heard because of the door that stood ajar, brought Christine out of her reminiscent trance. A new slew of curses from Colt Hansen upstairs was now directed at Carolyn for interfering in the argument with his wife.

"Shit," Liam said and put down the garbage bag he'd been filling. "Think we should help her out?"

Luke didn't stop for a second to think about it. He continued to pick up paper plates with half-eaten pieces of vanilla cake on them. "Carolyn's tougher than she looks. She's got this. It's not the first time she's stuck her nose in the middle of the Hansen's business. Ever since she called the cops on him last month, he usually checks himself. He mighta learned his lesson too if his wife hadn't bailed him out right away. Don't know why she did. She shoulda left him to rot. If I ever did that to my wife…ex-wife…she'da let me rot too. That's for sure."

A heavy silence hung in the room like a storm on the horizon. Christine couldn't imagine what it felt like to be hurt by someone she thought loved her. No matter what she did, she couldn't picture Liam ever raising a hand to her, even as an empty threat. He was a good, gentle man. If a bug got into the apartment, he was the one who cupped it in his hands and set it free out on the patio.

"Well, I'm going to head out while crazy is occupied," Luke said as he looked down at the gold watch on his wrist. It was half past midnight.

"Yeah, we're going to nod off now too." Liam tied the last garbage bag closed and tossed it by the door.

Christine dragged her feet along the beige carpet. Little pieces of shiny confetti stuck in between her toes. She peeled them from her feet, but when she tried to throw them away they stuck to her fingers. No amount of flailing freed them. "Dammit Allison," she mumbled as she shuffled off to the bedroom, still flicking her hands through the air. She sighed and tossed herself back onto the bed.

Liam stopped in the doorway and smiled at her. He'd never been so happy in his life.

III

Liam's phone beeped relentlessly early Sunday morning. At first he thought it was part of his dream, then a truck backing up in the parking lot outside their bedroom window, and finally the sound of an unread text message on his phone on the bedside table. He groaned and rolled over. It was a struggle to open his eyes as he rubbed the back of his hands over them. Everything was a blur.

He patted the table in search of his red-rimmed glasses and put them on. He blinked a few times to clear the sleep from his eyes and the remnants of his dreams. There was a red light blinking on his phone. When he pushed the button on the side, the time flashed. It was six-eighteen in the morning. He threw his head back and sighed. Despite his desire to drop the phone and go back to sleep, he read the message.

Dr. Hyde

Please come in to work today, as soon as you can. I have something important to tell you. There's still work to be done.

IV

Liam arrived at Valparaiso University at eight in the morning on the dot, like every work morning, though it was his day off. His legs moved swiftly as he rushed to Dr. Hyde's office as if he were gliding instead of walking.

Dr. Ronald Conrad joined his side from an adjoining hallway and tried to keep pace with him. "What's this all about?" he asked with perfectly rounded eyes.

"I don't know," Liam said through labored breaths as panic rose in his stomach. There couldn't be something wrong with the vaccine. It had worked. They did the trial. He saw it work.

Liam burst into his boss's darkened office. He stopped with his hand still on the doorknob. Ronald ran into his back, his hands up to brace the impact. The only source of light was a small lamp that gave off a dim orange glow. Behind the desk Dr. Hyde sat hunched over. A soft rattle emanated every time he took a breath. The movement of his shoulders was almost undetectable.

"Dr. Hyde," Liam said as his chest clenched at the sight of his boss. "Dr. Hyde, are you OK?" He rushed around the desk and bent down at his side.

Ronald stayed where he was with his hands on his hips as he tapped his foot. He did a small circle while he rubbed a hand over his blond hair to slick it back.

"The vaccine," Dr. Hyde huffed out through slightly parted, cracked lips. They were blue around the edges.

Liam bent in closer, his ear next to the doctor's mouth.

"No…good…" Dr. Hyde gave a hacking cough and struggled to raise his arm to place his hand over his mouth.

Liam looked at the desk and saw drops of blood splattered over the large, paper calendar. He took a deep breath.

"Call nine-one-one. Hurry!" Liam said to Ronald as he reached out to Dr. Hyde. "Just relax. Help is on the way," he said louder than he needed to. His heart beat twice its normal speed.

Dr. Hyde's breath slowed. It hissed from his chest with every exhale. "The trials…they're all…going…" he gasped. His pale blue eyes were distant.

Liam stood up straight and covered his mouth with one hand. His lips trembled. He turned to look at Ronald, who had taken a few steps out of the office to call the police, his back turned to them.

Dr. Hyde's body shook violently as he coughed again. The sound echoed through the office and down the hall. He threw himself forward, face-down, onto the desk as he struggled to breathe between fits of coughing. More blood flew from his lips to speckle the surface of the desk with red droplets.

"Oh, God, Dr. Hyde!" Liam said as he turned and bent over him again. He lightly touched the man's back to feel his chest wrack with force. "Dr. Hyde! Ronald, help!"

Ronald rushed in, but froze in the doorway. Dr. Hyde strained to take in air as blood oozed from the sides of his ivory lips. A puddle formed slowly under his face and crept outward. Then, all at once, the office fell silent.

Dr. Hyde lay still. He no longer gulped for air like a fish out of water. Blood reached the end of the desk and dripped over the side as Liam remained bent over him, frozen. He shook his head slowly, his eyes wet.

"My God," Ronald whispered. "Is he…?"

Liam didn't hear him. He couldn't hear anything. All his focus was on the now dead Dr. Hyde who lay across the desk, arms outstretched before him.

"Liam…Liam!" Ronald yelled, finally making his way across the office to put a hand to his friend's shoulder. He shook Liam from his stupor.

"We have to help him!" Liam yelled as he reached out to an inert Dr. Hyde. "We have to save him!"

Ronald pulled at Liam's shoulders as he struggled to grasp Dr. Hyde, sure that there was something he could do to bring him back. He swung his body to try and break free from Ronald's grip.

"He's gone, man. He's gone. There's nothing we can do. Look! He's gone," Ronald said as he threw his arms from Liam and gestured to Dr. Hyde.

Liam broke down. Death had played an important part in his life, but he'd never seen it up close before. He'd never seen the life of someone he knew extinguished before his eyes. His whole body shook as he tried to pull himself together. His knees wobbled as he stood up straight.

Ronald rested a hand on Liam's shoulder to lead him away from the dead man slumped over the desk.

"Wait," Liam said as he looked over his shoulder. "Do you hear that?"

Both men strained their ears, rooted where they stood, and leaned their bodies forward toward Dr. Hyde. A low rattle followed by a hissing wheeze grew in volume until there was no mistaking what it was.

"He's alive!" Liam yelled and rushed back over to the doctor. "Dr. Hyde, can you hear me? Are you OK?"

The doctor's fingers flexed and released. His nails scratched deeply into the wood of the desk. The rattling subsided and transformed into a low, rumbling growl from the depths of Dr. Hyde's throat.

Liam backed away slowly, hands held out in front of him as if his boss were a possibly rabid dog. The man clearly needed help. He didn't know why he was frightened. He should've given him CPR, but all he could think about was getting as far away from him as possible. He jumped when he felt the solidity of the door frame at his back.

"What the—" Ronald mumbled next to Liam, his head leaning forward as the rest of his body pressed against the wall.

Dr. Hyde's head moved from side to side in a jagged, broken motion. The growling built until it escaped his lips. Blood dripped from between his teeth as he lifted his head slowly. His eyes opened to reveal sickly yellowish-green irises veiled with a milky glaze, sunken in and surrounded by dark circles. As he stood up, his bones cracked like the popping of bubble wrap until he stood slackened with the desk in front of him. It was a small barrier between him and the two terrified doctors.

"No…fucking…way," Ronald whispered as his hands reached behind him to feel for the opening of the door.

Neither men wanted to make a move. Liam didn't know what they were looking at, but scrambling in a panic felt wrong, like painful and certain death. Liam wanted to say something to Dr. Hyde, sure that the man was lost and in some sort of pre-death shock, but nothing came out when he opened his mouth.

Dr. Hyde twisted his head slowly to the side like an animal assessing its prey. A moan escaped from between his red teeth. Liam gasped loudly and the doctor's head snapped to focus on the source of the sound. He wretched his mouth open and forced out a high cry as his feet dragged on the floor to move him alongside the desk and then forward. He gave a guttural growl with his arms outstretched, his stiff fingers flexed to grip the first thing they came in contact with.

Liam turned and fell through the doorway at top speed. "Come on!" he called out to Ronald, who ran as fast as he could but still fell behind Liam at lengths.

There was no thought of trying any of the other office doors to take shelter behind. No one had been there to unlock them since it was Sunday. All Liam saw in his mind was the pathway laid before him to the parking lot. He wasn't going to stop until he was in his car. His vision tunneled to the door at the end of the hallway that led to the reception area.

He looked over his shoulder when he heard Ronald cry out. His friend was spread across the floor and was trying to crawl in a scramble away from Dr. Hyde, who closed in on him. Ronald attempted to stand up, but slipped on the tile and fell back down onto his chest.

Liam stopped to face his friend. "Ronnie! Come on!"

Dr. Hyde threw himself down onto Ronald with his mouth wide-open.

"No!" Liam screamed, hunched over as his fingers pulled at his ginger hair. "Ronnie!"

Ronald reached out to Liam from down the hall as Dr. Hyde's jaw clenched the back of his neck. There was a blood curdling scream. Ronald's mouth opened and closed with silent gasps. Dr. Hyde tugged at him until he was on his back, face-up, to watch the horror he would behold. Nails dug into the helpless victim's face and shoulders and ripped the skin and muscles from the bones as his body jerked. Dr. Hyde groaned and his glazed eyes rolled back as he shoved flesh into his mouth. He chewed at it vigorously.

Liam couldn't move. He sobbed, repeating Ronald's name in a whisper as he watched in disgust and terror. His friend had just been torn apart before his eyes and he'd done nothing to stop it. What could he have done?

Once Ronald fell still, Dr. Hyde no longer dug into him. His head raised as his shark-like, dead eyes stared right at Liam. He pushed himself up off the ground and shambled down the hall towards the only live prey left.

Liam couldn't take his eyes away from what used to be his best friend lying broken and bleeding on the floor. He gurgled blood through his ripped throat and then, against all odds, rose slowly. Liam squeezed his eyes shut and opened them again. He was sure he had to be seeing things. Ronald stood in a pool of scarlet blood that dripped freshly from his wounds and down his pale blue button-up shirt. As he turned his gnarled face up to the ceiling, he let out an appalling shriek.

Ronald started forward and passed Dr. Hyde as Liam ran for the door. He pushed on it and moved the handle up and down to no avail. Somewhere in the depths of his memory he remembered he had to pull the door in order to open it. He shoved his way through just in time to miss the superhuman grip of Ronald's cold, dead hands.

Liam's breathing was labored as he ran at full speed out of the building and to his car. He let out gasping screams to the beat of his pounding feet. He felt his pockets for his keys and pulled them out, but the sweat in his eyes prevented him from seeing which button unlocked the doors. He pushed them all at random until he finally found the right one and heard the click as the locks popped up.

Meanwhile, Ronald and Dr. Hyde were closing in on him at a hauntingly slow pace. Every time Liam looked over his shoulder they were a few paces closer, their mouths open and stained with black, dried blood.

There was no one else around to help Liam. He was far into campus and students weren't permitted to go near the labs unless it was for class. He was all alone. He yanked open the door, shut himself inside, and slammed the palm of his hand down on the locks.

The thing that used to be Dr. Ronald Conrad made it to the car first and pressed itself against the window, pounding its fists into the glass. With each strike the window became streaked with dingy, darkened blood. The corpse of Dr. Hyde made its way over and followed Ronald's relentless attack on the car to get to the meat inside.

Liam's hands shook violently and he struggled to put the key into the ignition while jaws snapped at the air. Putrid eyes locked onto Liam's.

"This can't be happening," he repeated as he sat in the car, his eyes squeezed shut, the sound of dead fists beating against the window a distant sound in the background. Somewhere, he mustered up the strength and courage to step on the gas and drive away from what used to be his boss and friend. He looked over at the blood-streaked window and noticed a spidering crack. The sight sent a shiver down his neck and arms. He moved his eyes forward to the road as breathing in became harder for him to do.

www.ingramcontent.com/pod-product-compliance
Lightning Source LLC
Chambersburg PA
CBHW021955170726
47994CB00021B/412